UNSTOPPABLE
OCTOBIA
MAY

UNSTOPPABLE OCTOBIA MAY

SHARON G. FLAKE

SCHOLASTIC INC.

ISBN 978-0-545-79601-9

12 11 10 9 8 7 6 5 4 3   15 16 17 18 19 20/0

Printed in the U.S.A.   40

First Scholastic paperback printing, January 2015

The text was set in Bembo.

Book design by Nina Goffi

To my readers, the finest in the world. Thank you for walking this journey with me. May we always see the best in each another.

1

THE VAMPIRE IN ROOM 204

Vampires are not the nicest people. Maybe that happens when you live forever and don't get enough sun. So when I pass Mr. Davenport's bedroom door, I tiptoe, making my bare feet quiet as cotton balls tossed on the floor. Vampires can hear your thoughts and dreams, don't you know. So I'm not surprised when Mr. Davenport comes out wanting to kill me. I was dead once myself. I shouldn't let him scare me. But right now, I could wet my britches.

Green veins sit on top of his feet. His toes twist and curl, and his yellow toenails need tending; that's what I notice. Then I see them. Fangs. Long as the hound's teeth that bit my uncle's two middle fingers off. "If you come in my room again I'll —" He's running up the hall, stepping in the spot I made yesterday when I tried to wash my cat, Juppie, with Lucky Tiger hair tonic for men. It makes her fur shine.

Mr. Davenport steps on the back of my heel and I trip. Fingers that feel like crab claws dig into my arm, pinching, pulling me so close I can smell his sour breath burning my eyelashes off, practically. I try to scream. But the words get stuck in my throat. His fangs get closer and closer to my neck, tasting my blood, I bet, before they even break the skin.

"Don't make me come up there, girl!" Aunt Shuma is standing at the bottom of the steps.

He stops. His bloodshot eyes staring into mine. When he whispers, his voice is softer than a spider walking across a feather. "I could kill you . . . if I wanted." His hands hold on to my throat, squeezing.

"Mr. Davenport. You okay?" Aunt Shuma's not worried about me. Just him, the boarder who pays the most rent of anyone living here — fifteen dollars a week. "I try to keep her away but she wants to be a writer, too, like you. And solve mysteries like that Nancy Drew. Terrible imagination she got. Girl — come!"

As quick as a blink, he is at the other end of the hall, by his door, wiping his fingers on his flannel pants like he was touching something dirty when he had his hands on me. "I want it back." His words are in my head, not in the air for my ears to hear. His fangs disappear. And he turns me loose. "It belongs to me. And I'll get it back from you. One way or another."

Holding my neck, I warn him like he's warning me. "Everybody will know about you, even President Eisenhower. Negroes helped elect him, you know. So I wrote to him about you." Right then I wonder why my garlic did not protect me. Out the corner of my eyes, I see the sun coming up. Daylight ought to kill him, or at least send him running. "What kind of vampire are you?"

He smiles. "I write books. Don't you know?" Then he disappears.

Running upstairs. Jumping into the bed. And crossing myself. I reach under my pillow to grab the jar of cut-up garlic I keep in my room because my aunt says if I keep eating the big, whole cloves, she will put me out like she did the rabbits I snuck in once.

Eating a few pieces, I hop out of bed and pull a chair across the room to stand on. As careful as a mother bird carrying her young, I pick up Mr. Davenport's ring. When I took it from his room, I hid it on the top shelf of my closet in the box that holds Auntie's blue satin pillbox hat. I knew he would never look for it there.

Sometimes after everyone goes to sleep, I sit outside Mr. Davenport's room waiting for him to come home from doing his vampire work. I always fall asleep, so of course Auntie must carry me to bed. Last night was different. A girl crying inside his room woke me before Auntie did. I had a pointy stick when I went inside his room. Checking underneath his bed and behind the curtains, I tried my best to find her. Just before I left I heard her say, "Octobia May." She even knew my last name. "Help me."

"Where are you?" I said, stepping into the big cedar closet. Standing face-to-face with his army uniform, I saluted sadly. Mr. Davenport fought in World War II a few years ago. Before Dracula and his friends got to him and turned him evil.

I tried my best to rescue her, but I couldn't find her anywhere. I did find a dollar. Plus two twenty-dollar bills balled up in a corner. I only went into his jacket pockets to see how rich he was. That's when I found the ring.

I saw my first ever vampire movie in October — one of the months I'm named after. I turned ten and finally Auntie said I was old enough to go to the drive-in movies on monster night. We saw *Abbott and Costello Meet Frankenstein* and *House of Dracula*. The next evening — he moved in.

It took me a long time to recognize him for what he is. I think that's because Mr. Davenport is colored like me. In comic books and movies, the vampires are all white. Now I know the truth — vampires do not discriminate. Any race is welcome to join their club.

2

A SWITCH AND A GOOD TONGUE-LASHING

"Octobia May. Stop pestering Mr. Davenport and get down here. Now!"

I used to pretend I could not hear in my bedroom on the third floor, but my aunt would come to my room anyhow. She'd be even madder and punish me longer. So I learned, come down fast as you are able and get it over with. And bring garlic. No, eat it, more than usual. She ain't no vampire, but she hates the stuff.

Aunt Shuma points to the front door. I push open the screen and walk outside, picking up Juppie. "Switches. Why is she always making me pull switches?"

From Auntie's porch steps, I watch the vegetable man's horse turning the corner. Then the last of his red wooden wagon disappearing. One by one I snap off branches from a low-hanging tree, and look up at the gas lamp that lights our street. Sliding the leaves off the branches, I wonder when we'll have electric lights like most everyone else in town.

I'm back in the kitchen in a flash. Auntie's at the stove stewing tomatoes and frying catfish and fatback. Pouring hominy into hot water. Stirring navy beans in her favorite pot. She urges me to crack some eggs. She thinks you are lazy if you do one thing at a time. Knitting while she's cooking, both breakfast and supper, makes sense to her. Playing with my paper dolls and doing homework doesn't.

I sit five switches on the chair. She leaves the wooden spoon standing in the pot of beans. I close my eyes and hold out both hands. You'd think she'd want to be saved from a vampire, not just smile at him because his rent's paid up for one whole year. Auntie turns the radio down. "Now why is it wrong to go into other people's rooms?"

I squeeze my eyes tight. "Everyone has a right to their private things and private thoughts." I am repeating what she taught me. "But . . ."

I feel the switches. I hear her telling me that vampires "ain't real and Mr. Davenport is a writer, not a

6

vampire who came back from the dead and is trying to make us all into vampires, too."

I open my eyes and stare at the switches sitting in my hand like lamb's ear. "Why do I have to pull these, if you never use 'em?"

She walks over to the stove and takes out the spoon. "I might just use something else, Miss Too Much Mouth. Now get over here."

My mouth opens wide, and then it's warm and full inside. "Vampires . . ." I quit talking so I can finish chewing.

"Jesus, don't you stink." She pinches her nose, opens the oven, and smiles at her blueberry pie. She asks how it can be possible for a girl to wake up smelling like three boys playing in the sun at high noon. I mention vampires again and she says, "There's no such thing. Werewolves and vampires are just stories people make up to sell books and get you to the picture show. Anyhow, who ever seen a colored vampire? It would be like saying men can walk on the moon." She really laughs then.

"I bet there are Chinese vampires; probably Jewish ones, too," I tell her. Sitting at the table, I try to explain what I know. They can come in all colors. It's just . . . well, they started overseas so they mostly come in white. I smell my breath. I think the garlic's wearing off. "Why do you think he never goes out in the daytime?" I pick up the salt box. Pouring salt over both shoulders. "He'll die if he does." I remember what happened earlier. Him up and about while the sun was out. *Are all vampires the same?* I ask myself. *Or do some make up their own rules like Auntie says I do?*

She tells me that I am getting too old for such foolishness. "Besides . . . don't you hear him up there on that typewriter?" She walks over to the icebox and takes out butter. She made it like she makes everything. "Imagine a writer living under our very own roof."

I imagine myself writing. Surrounded by lots of books all written by me. It's a silly thought, my friend Jonah thinks. I'd better satisfy myself with being a wife when I grow up, he sometimes tells me. Taking in laundry, drawing my husband's bath.

Auntie leaves the room, returning with Mr. Davenport still on her mind. She brings up all the times I said something was real and true when it was me making things up.

If I were pretending, would I write a letter to President Eisenhower? I shook his hand last year when I went home to Pittsburgh to visit. He was at the Pennsylvania train station courting votes. Mom and Dad still have their I LIKE IKE signs at our house, too. Aunt Shuma tells me that the president is too busy trying to end communism and make the Koreans behave to be bothered with my shenanigans. She may be right. He never wrote me back.

"You rise early to help me feed all these folks. Not to help yourself to another tall tale." Besides, she says, why aren't I trying to put my mind to thinking on more useful things? Like what I can do to help those poor kids down south. "They don't have it nearly as good as we do up north."

Sitting at the table, she picks up the newspaper. I turn up the radio and sing along with Miss Patti Page. "How much is that doggie in the window? Arf, arf."

"Octobia May."

I imagine that I am standing in front of Mr. Silverman's appliance store window watching television. All ten sets are turned to the *I Love Lucy* show. One day I hope we get a TV set. Auntie says she never will. Television is a fad, like station wagons and poodle skirts, she thinks.

Auntie turns to her favorite section of the paper, the obituaries. "Lordy," she says. I pull a chair up to hers. "Look who done ended up dead in Bend River. Randy Mars, the chef for the president of S and L Bank." She nudges me. In his old life, Auntie tells me, Mr. Mars ran numbers for the mob. "Guess it caught up to him."

She reads out loud, like we don't have enough death around here already. Then she talks about the bank. Wondering if she shouldn't try to get a loan there. Almost every bank in town has turned her down. "It's nineteen fifty-three. Everything is changing. Time for women to get a piece of the pie, too."

Slowly I crack and stir brown eggs into a yellow glass bowl that Auntie earned with her Green Stamps. And ponder over poor old Mr. Mars. Would he rather be dead in the ground letting moles and fire ants eat him or be a blood-sucking vampire like Mr. Davenport? Dead but still alive.

3

BASEMENT SECRETS

I tried to tell my mother not to send me here to live. Besides the graveyard around the corner, there's the Sunrise Funeral Parlor two blocks over. The undertaker is always asking how I'm doing. Like he hopes I'll get sick again and come to be with him soon. My mother sent me anyhow. Even after I cried and made myself throw up.

After I died, my mother changed. Treating me like a teacup she was scared of breaking. I could stay in the house. Or sit in the rocker in the shade on the porch. But I could not go to school. Or play with other children. Polio or tuberculosis — I could catch them, she worried. Or maybe someone, "God forbid," would sneeze and that would be the end of me, she thought.

Running and skipping rope with my three sisters was done with, too. Even church and the choir she made me join was over with. Not that I minded. Church three days a week — twice on Saturday and all day Sunday — brought out the devil in me.

It was Aunt Shuma's idea to come to live with her two years ago. "'Cause there's more than one way to die." She wrote that in her letter to Momma and Daddy, promising to keep me away from those snotty-nosed kids at school. She was only joshing. Now Auntie says I better not make her sorry for all the freedom she's given me. "A girl in this day and time," she likes to tell me, "is as free as people let her be." So she let me be, and my heart healed and my feet found out that freedom is as big as the moon for a colored gal who ain't afraid of nothing.

"Octobia May. Towels." Auntie puts away the last breakfast dish and orders me to the basement for clean towels. I run upstairs first. Putting on one of her house-dresses. The longest I can find.

I take Auntie's best hat — the one with the ring on top — and carefully sit it in the middle of a basket. Carrying the basket on my head, I walk down the wooden spiral stairs. Twisting like loose brown curls, they take me to the cellar, where Auntie says servants used to work. Sometimes I pretend to be one of them. Not today. I've got to hide Mr. Davenport's ring. He'll find it for sure if I dawdle.

"This morning," I tell my pretend servant friends, "he tried to kill me. For this." I hold up the ring. It has the silhouette of a girl's face and shoulders on it. "And look," I say to them. "Initials. Not his." I search the basement for a hiding place. Starting with the fallout shelter near the corner by the coal bin. That's the place Auntie says we're to run if the communists fly to America and drop radiation bombs on us.

Soon I am back where I started, at the front of the basement standing beside Auntie's casket. Sitting the hat and ring inside, I circle them three times with Morton Salt. "My friends will look after you," I tell the girl on the ring. Closing the lid, I sprinkle salt on that, too. It keeps bad spirits away.

The man who used to own the graveyard up the street owned this house, too. Then my aunt bought it and found all that he was hiding — caskets and headstones, fingers and thumbs, and skulls, too. Nobody lived here for almost thirty-five years. When she bought it, sight unseen, for just about nothing, she didn't know what she was getting, Auntie likes to say. The bones went into the ground up the street. The caskets were sold — except the one Auntie kept. She says one day it'll be her sleeping away in it.

"Shoo." Juppie has been underfoot since I came downstairs. I do not think she likes caskets.

From the top of the stairs, Auntie warns me. "Octobia May. You are not a servant. Or whatever you pretending to be down there. Just be you for once," she begs. "And bring me up those towels!"

I pull towels off the line as fast as I am able. Clothespins bounce off my forehead, hit my cat, and hop high off the floor like grasshoppers. Tripping on Auntie's dress, I head for the steps, waving at the servants and thinking about home. Momma had me in a cage. Now I am free.

I wag my finger at my pretend friends, asking them to repeat what Auntie taught me. "Freedom is something people try to give you sparingly. 'Cause once you got it, you do with your life what you will."

My parents volunteer with the NAACP, so they feel that way, too. But at our house, girls are the least free Negroes. Mother and Father say there will be a time and a place for us girls to get everything that's ours. Auntie believes that the time for girls to be free is now.

It is nice to be free. Nice to come and go. To even hunt for vampires late at night if you want. But on my way upstairs, I think about the children Auntie says I should think of more often. Wondering what they do for fun on a hot summer's day.

4

A NEW GIRL ON THE BLOCK

"You don't come into my room when I'm gone, do you?" Mr. Buster, our favorite boarder, rubs my head on his way past. He heard Mr. Davenport and me this morning, I suppose.

I settle myself on the parlor floor to fold clothes. "I do not go in nobody's room."

My friend Jonah disagrees, saying that once I went into his mother's bedroom while she was taking her Saturday bath. She has not liked me much since, he tells him.

I fold another towel, thinking about all the feet and fingers that get dried on it. Ears, too. Mr. Piers blows his nose on them when he thinks no one is looking. That's why I wear wool gloves when I help Auntie wash.

Mr. Buster sits down in the burgundy smoking chair underneath the stained glass windows. Cranked open wide, they blow the curtains and send a warm breeze around the room. "That man. I saw him in that casket once." He looks up at the ceiling.

Juice from a tomato drips down the corner of Jonah's mouth, like vampire blood. Standing in our garden, talking through the open window, he advises Mr. Buster against bringing up devils and vampires. "'Cause she will believe you."

"Are you sure it was Mr. Davenport?" I ask.

Mr. Buster packs his pipe with tobacco. "Sure as I am that your aunt's the best cook in town." He winks.

I think about the ring. *What if Mr. Davenport goes to the basement and tries to steal it?* I stand up. From the dining room, Auntie tells me to sit and finish folding. How can I? I have to rescue the girl.

Jonah comes inside, wiping his hands on his pants. Mr. Buster sticks a pipe in his mouth and opens the newspaper. He's looking for a new job. A Negro can have his choice of any one he likes in this day and age, he believes. Of course Jonah wants the baseball section. Satchel Paige is his favorite player. But Jackie Robinson and the Dodgers are the talk of the town.

"They hiring at the funeral parlor, I see." Mr. Buster folds the paper in half. "Pays good money . . . and you don't get back talk from nobody." He laughs. "Get it? . . . No . . . body."

Dead is all around me, which is why I go into the kitchen for more garlic. "They smell funny . . . people who work in those places," I tell him once I get back.

"The true benefit," he says, "is that you get a discount when it's your time to go." He smiles when he slides his finger under his throat.

I open the newspaper. *New homes. Apartments for rent. Efficiencies*, the ads say. *Sixty-five dollars a month. Working man or woman with pleasing lifestyle wanted.* I let Auntie know she can buy a bathtub for fifteen dollars.

Auntie walks in, fluffing pillows. "Why do I want that?"

A house like ours is listed, too. Thirteen rooms. Three bathrooms. Ten thousand five hundred dollars. "Keep talking." Auntie tugs at her bibbed apron. Mr. Buster compliments her hair. Pin curled the evening before, it looks full and shiny.

Jonah takes another section of the paper, and then gives Auntie and me some good news. We'll be getting new neighbors. He even shows me their address in the paper. "Now I'll have a real live girl to play with," he says. Bessie is her name. Her mother is having a baby.

Her father will teach at our school. I wonder if I will be in his class.

Stories start to fill my head like air in a balloon. Bessie and I will be best friends. Her father will walk her and me to school every morning. Walk us home each day for lunch. Sitting down a towel, I think about Mr. Davenport. Was he ever a husband and father? Was he a good soldier during the war?

Jonah lights the pipe. Mr. Buster blows a thick ring of smoke and looks at the ceiling. "That man. I seen blood dripping out of the side of his mouth once. She right to watch him, otherwise . . ." His finger slides under his neck again. "I might just see her at my next job, if they got enough smarts to hire me, that is."

I eat a piece of peeled garlic I stuck in my pocket and finish folding clothes. Mr. Buster would like me to back up a bit. Jonah pinches his nose before going to the window for air.

Aunt Shuma waits for the grandfather clock in the foyer to quit chiming before she asks Mr. Buster to please not make her life no harder by stirring my imagination up. He doesn't get the chance to answer. Our other boarders are making their way downstairs. Using canes and holding on to the walls, Mrs. Loewenthal and Mrs. Ruby are singing "Happy Days Are Here Again."

I join in. We all do for a while.

5

WAR AND OTHER TROUBLES

"Afternoon, Octobia May." For a quarter a week, Mr. Piers gives me organ lessons. I'd rather play the piano. But the organ came with the house. Interrupting him, Mrs. Loewenthal brings up my crochet lessons. I played stickball with Jonah yesterday and skipped it. I give her my word I will be there later today. Then I ask Auntie for permission to go to the basement. Standing behind me kneading my shoulders, she is ignoring me. Asking our boarders about their aches and pains, instead.

Mrs. Ruby comes down last, her ruby-red shoes sparkling like Dorothy's in *The Wizard of Oz*. The cane she uses is from Ireland. Her husband was a college professor at Lincoln University and they went there once. "Open your own bank account. Even in secret. Otherwise your husband may spend all the money and you won't know anything until he is deceased and you are a widow living hand to mouth in someone else's home."

I am thinking about vampires. Not husbands. Walking into the dining room beside me, she compliments Auntie on "another lovely feast."

Everyone takes a seat at the table except him, who never eats with us, by the way. I tell Auntie it's because vampires cannot eat people food. Of course she doesn't believe me. Now she has them all talking about him and how he saved someone during the war. Mrs. Loewenthal pinches my cheek. "A true American hero."

I light the candles. Jonah turns the radio on low. Mr. Nat King Cole sings "Mona Lisa" and sets Mr. Buster's foot to tapping.

Auntie finishes filling my glass with sassafras tea. Mr. Buster gets back to the war. It's been over eight years, but the grown-ups say they'll never forget it. Maybe because everyone lost someone in the war. I lost an uncle I never met. Mr. Buster lost his wife. She did not like having a husband so far away and found herself a new one. Mrs. Loewenthal brings up her grandfather and the two spinster aunts she lost. They died in concentration camps.

"That Hitler." I cover my mouth because I do not like to speak his evil name. He killed so many people. I get sad when I think about it. But lucky her. Her family escaped.

"You and your husband mind washing all them dishes?" Jonah knows the story by heart. "If I was a college teacher I wouldn't want to do that."

I think about my father.

In Germany, her husband was a college professor. Then everything changed. They escaped, though, to Sweden. Writing letters to colleges here. "Such jobs were in short support. Lots of colleges in this country would not hire Jews." But they came anyway. She cooked. He took a job as a butler. And kept writing letters. Lincoln University. A Negro college said yes. "Come. We can use a good teacher like you." Mrs. Loewenthal reaches for Mrs. Ruby's hand. "They treated us like family at that university. The students write to me still."

It's Auntie who lightens our mood. "Cheer up. 'Cause everybody at this table done earned the right to some good times." She mentions the Depression, World War II, and the millions of people those Nazis killed. Jim Crow and the Korean War, too.

"Who's Jim Crow?" Jonah whispers.

Auntie lifts her glass. We all do. "Cheers!" She stands. "Here's to good jobs and all that we want in life." She says America is on the right track and things are looking up for everybody.

Jonah jumps up. "I want to shake Satchel Paige's hand."

Mrs. Loewenthal is happy again. "Then it will happen, Jonah. Believe."

I stand up for Auntie. "Somebody will give you that loan. I know it!"

Everyone is singing it now, "Happy Days Are Here Again," including Jonah, who marches around the table using a spatula as a baton, singing louder than the rest. But it's when the singing is done that we all hear it.

Tick. Tap. Tap. Tap, tick, tap . . . tick.

Everyone stares at the ceiling. The noise is coming from his room.

He's awake. Typing in the daylight — which he never does. We are quiet for a bit. But not him. Busy as a bee in a bonnet, he worries the keys. And me.

"What's on your mind, Octobia May?" Mr. Buster holds up a bowl filled with Brussels sprouts and winks. "Vegetables or vampires?"

They all laugh. Even Miss Marble, who sat in the parlor with me Thursday evening and would not turn my hand loose when Mr. Davenport shimmied down the fire escape steps and hurried up the block, wearing a trench coat and fedora hat when the night was hot. And the moon was full.

"Evil's got this way about it," Miss Marble told me. "Having toast at somebody else's table one morning. Sitting at the foot of your bed, come nightfall."

Mrs. Loewenthal asks me to tell everyone a story. "But no vampires. No monsters. I do not approve of that kind of talk." Because of her family, blood and devil stories make her very nervous.

She sets a nickel by my fork. Mr. Buster places a dime beside it. Jonah's penny adds to the pile, by the time I finish the story.

Following supper, I rush down the stairs, begging my dress not to trip me. "Did he come?" I ask the servants. "Is it still here?"

Jonah walks over to the furnace, kicking around coals that fell from the bin. I point to my pretend servant friends, roasting squirrels on the spit. Sweating from all the heat.

I open the lid, slowly. Juppie meows louder than ever before. Lifting the hat, I let them all see. "It's gone."

6

GRAVEYARD KISSES

At the bottom of the fence they put sharp, pointy spikes meant to keep people out. The daggers pull at my new poodle skirt. Ripping a hole in my crinoline slip. But I keep sliding underneath the fence anyhow.

Jonah lays on the ground next. "Hate graveyards." He slides under the fence close behind me. "What if a ghost —"

I tug at my skirt and slip. "If you want to fight vampires, you can't be afraid of anything."

He pokes his lips out and tells me to pay up.

The boys on Jonah's street are collecting kisses. The

one who gets the most wins ten nickels. Jonah is a runt. Plus his left eye is crooked, always staring at his nose. No girl wants to kiss him. But I thought up a way he can still win. Get all his kisses from me. I'll give him his kisses tonight in the graveyard, underneath the crescent moon. I promised him seven. So far no one has collected more than five.

I shine the flashlight in Jonah's eyes on purpose. "Quit that." He crosses his hands in front of his face like Dracula does when silver bullets or crucifixes are too close. "You just don't wanna kiss me. Okay. I'll leave, then. Right now. I swear."

I am not afraid to be in the graveyard alone. But I need Jonah to help me prove that Mr. Davenport is a real-life vampire. Running over to him, I bump my lips on his. He fans his nose. "If you don't quit with the garlic, Octobia May, you won't have no friends at all."

I stick my lips out. "Want another kiss?"

He smiles and shakes his head yes.

"Well, get it from a girl who don't stink." I am skipping up the path. Listening to my Mary Jane shoes say hello to every rock and brick they touch, when Jonah catches up to me. Quietly. We walk under the stars and look up at the moon. I stop and point. "That's a crescent moon, Jonah. Auntie says they're lucky." Birds talk in the trees like it's early morn and they are making plans for their day. One flies past my face, almost taking my nose off.

"That's a sign, Octobia May. Bad luck's coming."

I squeeze his hand and offer to share my garlic. Then together we walk up my favorite lane. The one that twists and turns like a spinning top. The longer we walk, the blacker it gets out. Soon trees block the streetlights and cut the moon in half. Things we can't see run across the grass. Or shilly-shally up trees. At the fountain in front of the crematory, I pull up my slip and scratch my thighs. Crinoline slips are wide and puffy, like wedding cakes. But as easy on a girl as glass in her slippers.

Jonah turns his back to me. "Jeepers creepers, Octobia May. A boy shouldn't see your underthings."

I walk up the road, pointing out the people I know. On this side there is a family of four sisters who passed one year after the next. I call them the Before Girls. The last one passed in 1865. I make up stories about them. "They came north with their father and mother," I tell Jonah, "walking behind a horse-drawn wagon. Following the North Star." Auntie says they didn't bury Negroes in this cemetery until recently. Jews, either. I think they should have, so I tell my story my own way.

Walking between gravestones and shadows, Jonah wonders about the crows in the trees sitting like people on pews. He shines light all around us. "Are you sure a

crescent moon is a lucky moon? Because I wanna win."
He wipes sweat off his skinny nose. "I never win,
Octobia May. Do I?"

Jonah is always the first to lose at marbles. The last
one picked for stickball. "No, Jonah. You never win.
But if you help me prove Mr. Davenport is a vampire,
you won't have to win nothing anymore. That will be
the biggest prize of all."

Jonah sticks his fingers in both his ears. "My mother
don't believe in vampires, Octobia May. She says —"

I stomp my foot. "Your mother doesn't believe in
girls wearing pants, either, does she, Jonah? She said it
was unseemly, me wearing slacks on a Sunday." Jonah's
mother warned me. If I did not change my outfit so I
looked like a decent, self-respecting colored gal, he
could not come out and play with me today. So I am
wearing this skirt for him. He is at Everlasting Peace
Cemetery after midnight for me and seven kisses.

At the top of the hill, I step out of my slip. Swinging
it like a lasso, I send it into the trees. Afterward I kiss
Jonah on the cheek ten times; each side. Not so he'll
win. So he'll win big.

He rubs both his cheeks. "I feel it, Octobia May. I
feel myself shining inside bright as all those nickels I'm
gonna win."

"We'll both win, Jonah. Watch and see."

I am happy, whistling, when Jonah repeats what the

old folks say. A whistling girl and a crowing hen always come to a no-good end.

His words are barely out of his mouth before a crow flies overhead fast and low. Black as midnight, it pulls some of my hairs out along the way.

7

A NIGHT FOR VAMPIRES

Jonah and I walk. And walk. Till we get to the part of the cemetery where the storm still lives. Broken trees. Cracked headstones. Caskets lifted out the ground. Jonah quits walking when he sees it all. Auntie's flashlight tries to quit, too. "Octobia May. I — I think I hear my mother calling me." He backs up slowly.

Hurricanes never do come to this city, they say. But the day after *he* came to live here, two showed up, one behind the other. The river drowned bridges. Floods swallowed up houses and stores. Trees old as the city fell easy as rice off a fork. In some places, like the graveyard, you can still see it.

Jonah is turning in circles. Shining the flashlight on a bulldozer, at graves, over the grass, and up and down trees bent to leaning. Not too far away is a grave, fresh dug. Stepping up to the edge, we both stare inside. I tell Jonah about the girl on the ring.

"Octobia May." He shakes his head. "Maybe Mr. Davenport is a Mason, and that is most likely his secret ring."

"A vampire cannot be a Mason. You have to be alive to be in that club. Anyhow, what if he did magic and trapped her on it?"

My imagination, he says, will get my mouth washed out with soap one day for sure. He brings up Bessie, the new girl. He thinks she might be just what I need. To end my talking to the dead and "conjuring up vampire devils."

Taking giant steps, I lead him over to where they laid Mr. Davenport's body long before even my great-grandfather was born. "It's a mausoleum, Jonah — an apartment for the dead." I wave him over. I found it the other day while I was playing. Part of the roof is smashed in. The front door is missing; so is the casket. I kick away an empty Chesterfield pack. Stepping on piles of leaves and broken sticks, I stop. Then, together, Jonah and I walk inside.

I shine light on the leaky walls. And read. *Risen.*

"The word is written in blood." Jonah says it's red crayon. He tries to rub it off with his fist.

"It'll never disappear," I tell him. Quiet as a prayer in church, I read the moldy green nameplate screwed into the wall. "H. Willard Davenport the eighth. Born eighteen seventy. Died nineteen ten. Pneumonia." Facing Jonah, I feel like a winner, too. "See, Jonah? He's dead and alive."

Using his pitching arm, he throws a pretend ball and hits it with an invisible bat. "This is nineteen fifty-three, Octobia May. The Yankees gonna win the World Series, much as I wish they wouldn't. That's the gosh darn truth. What you saying is another story you made up." He smacks the nameplate, and it falls off. "Don't know why I came. I keep getting whooped because of you. . . ." He takes off running.

All through the graveyard, Jonah and I stick as close to one another as words on a headstone. We rest after a while and then make our way up top to where the Before Girls are. I introduce Jonah to them. He shakes his head. Fanning them with the bottom of my skirt I ask if they are warm tonight. He says I have screws in my head. "Those girls are dust and dirt like everyone else here." Later Jonah holds the flashlight so I can slide underneath the fence.

Standing up on the other side, I mention Mr. Davenport again. "Colored or not, a vampire is not a good thing to have living in your house, Jonah."

He asks why I am so bothered by him now since he's lived with us for months. Like a hibernating bear, I kept to myself. Watching him and recording his ways. Then spring came, and I knew what I had to do. "Good detectives take their time, Jonah."

Jonah dallies. I search the ground for four-leaf clovers in soft dirt along the fence. Pointing to soldiers' graves, he salutes. "Aye, aye, sailors." And mentions the little flags newly planted beside their headstones. "Octobia May, did you put —"

"Hush. Listen." The birds are louder than before. Screaming like monkeys at the zoo, they fly high over our heads. "Turn the flashlight this way, Jonah. We need to see what's over there."

He laughs. "Look." He's pointing to rabbits at the end of the fence. "Wish I had my BB gun. Pow. Into the pot they'd go." He brags about giving each of his friends a lucky rabbit's foot.

I hear shoes walking fast, breaking sticks. "Someone else is out here, Jonah. Give me that flashlight."

He lies on the ground to crawl underneath the fence. Then up he jumps like a jack-in-the-box. "Vampires." He beats his chest with both fists like Tarzan. "Can't win against me." He winks when he looks my way.

"This was fun, Octobia May. Glad I came. Maybe. Hey. Don't — Nooo!"

I rip Jonah's shirtsleeve, trying to hold on to him. The flashlight drops when he gets dragged away. Jonah begs. "Please . . . don't kill me. Please."

The spikes cut my belly when I crawl under this time. Running in the dark, I try to reach my friend. When I see Mr. Davenport leaning over Jonah's neck to bite him, I close my eyes. And scream. "Help! Help! A vampire is killing my friend!"

8

A DISGRACE TO THE
NEIGHBORHOOD

Some things you just should tell a kid. Like when a man that's living with you gets a job working the night shift at the graveyard.

"Tell you that for what?" Aunt Shuma asks. "If you quit spying and sneaking and . . ."

I sit up in bed holding tight to the cross Miss Marble gave me as soon as I came home. "How could you believe him? He never had a job, not in all the time he's been living here."

Auntie tells me that if I do not quit this madness

she'll use those switches on me for sure. She feels bad about that, I think. So she pulls up my nightshirt again and wipes the scratches on my stomach with peroxide. Swallowing, she asks if my chest hurts. What she really wants to know is if my heart is okay.

I lean back on my elbows. "I can never die."

"Once was surely enough," she says. Her lips move, but I can't hear all that she is saying. I know it's about me and vampires and her having a headache. But if it wasn't for me, Aunt Shuma would be dead or a vampire herself. She doesn't know, but I stuck a wooden cross under the newspaper that lines her jewelry-box drawer. I put a paper one at the bottom of her purse, under the small hammer she keeps there. There are others in the house, but I'd never say where.

"Do you know what woulda happened if Officer O'Malley didn't see us, Auntie?" I am holding my throat, right where Mr. Davenport could have bit it. "Jonah would be dead. Me too."

She reaches for the bottle of cod liver oil, forcing two spoonfuls into my mouth. "Give that man some peace, child. Let him do his job at the graveyard."

"I thought you said he was a writer." I wipe my lips. She picks up a book. She promised my parents she'd read to me every night. I think they meant for her to read animal stories and fairy tales. But lots of times she reads me *Little Women* or Nancy Drew — books she bought years back when she worked at a uniform factory, helping out with the war effort.

Now she has second thoughts, she says, leaving and returning with the Pittsburgh edition of the *Courier*. It has all the stories about Negroes in my hometown and the rest of the country, too. Maybe, she says, if I heard more real, true stories, it would settle my mind some. "Look, see? Another school in the South is in trouble. Thank God for Thurgood Marshall and the NAACP. They just went to the Supreme Court again. They'll make 'em set all these wrongs right."

I am thinking about Mr. Davenport. Did he fly home or walk? "And if he's working all night and sleeping all day, when does he have enough time to write?" I ask her.

Aunt Shuma doesn't lift her head or stop reading or turning pages.

"If I was a writer —"

"You are not a writer!"

I crawl from underneath the covers and walk across the room. With my hand full of papers and notebooks from the hope chest she says she'll never use — I walk over to her. Some of my stories are about him. Others are about Jonah and me. Or my family in Pittsburgh. I read a page. Auntie's mood changes. Now she seems as loose and easy as the linen drapes hanging at my windows.

She supposes that a writer is simply someone who writes, and tells me I must be one, too, then.

I've been digging through the trash, I tell her. He never throws out anything — not food, or words, not even soap. "Do vampires wash?" I put my things away. "Does he use deodorant? Brush his teeth?" I cover my mouth. "Don't you wonder about things like that, Aunt Shuma?"

She takes me by the shoulders and gently makes me lay down. "He pays his rent. So I don't care who he bites or what he do and don't write." She begins to read the *Courier*. The choir at my home church is sending new books and new pencils to a school in Arkansas. Their books are old and tattered. The building sometimes leaks from rain.

My school is warm and clean. Both colored children and whites go there. But every year Auntie says it's changing. Only five people that look like Mrs. Loewenthal live on our block now. "Can I send pencils?"

Auntie hugs me. "Yes. Truly. It's a real thing that you can do for real children."

She doesn't answer when I say I'll send a few of my stories, too. She sets the paper down and tucks me in. "Sleep well."

But how can I with so many thoughts in my head? I catch her when she's practically out my door. "I need to talk to you, Auntie." Sitting up, I undo her hard work.

She turns as prickly as a porcupine. "Octobia May! Go to sleep!"

When I start to cry, Auntie comes to hold me. Asking what the trouble is. No one believes me. And she said she would always hear me out, I say. But now . . . Sitting beside me, she unties the white satin ribbons in my hair. And lays them on my night table. Give her the story once more, she says, pinching my cheek. "Maybe there is a stitch of something true in it."

I start with Officer O'Malley, who found us at the graveyard. It was my screaming that drew him to us, I tell Auntie. But Mr. Davenport is as good at making up stories as I am. He told Officer O'Malley that it was his first day on the job. And that he found me and Jonah breaking in or busting out the cemetery. I told Jonah to show Officer O'Malley his bite marks. Only he didn't have any. So I said, tell him how he almost bit you. Mr. Davenport must have erased Jonah's memory, I tell Auntie. "He could not remember anything except my kisses."

She reaches for the cod liver oil, this time for herself.

I show her the way Officer O'Malley tipped his hat good night to Mr. Davenport. "It's a crescent moon out, Octobia May," he said to me. "Strange things can occur on a fine night like this. And monsters aplenty can rise in an imagination like yours."

I ask Auntie if she knew Officer O'Malley was Irish. "Who doesn't?" she says.

"He believes in leprechauns and shamrocks. He told me so once himself. But not vampires." I lay back. "You believe in leprechauns, Auntie?"

Holding my hands in hers, she tells me about the time she tried to fly. She sat on the edge of a tin roof. Sheets tied around her stomach. The other end knotted to the bedpost. "I jumped, thinking the wind would catch me."

A colored doctor came to the house. Sewed her knee up, set her broken fingers and stitched her forehead. "Keep spinning tales, Octobia May. And you will surely fall down and break something, too."

I think about what Jonah's mother said. "Auntie — do you think I give the Negro race a bad name?"

After Officer O'Malley took Jonah home, Mrs. Nicholson said I was improper. Out late at night without a slip. My dress ripped. Girls like me with no self-respect or decorum give us all a bad name, she told me.

"You are a top-notch student. A credit. No disgrace."

I squeeze her hard with my hug. "I do not think you give the Negro race a bad name, either."

She looks surprised.

"Jonah's mother said unmarried spinsters are a bad thing, too."

Auntie's temper shows sometimes. "Colored or white. Married or an old maid. A woman in this world can't play banjo to nobody's fiddle. She's got to be her own one-and-only true self, Octobia May." Standing tall over me, she folds her arms.

"Like you, Auntie?"

"Yes. Like me."

"And me. Walking in graveyards. Writing about vampires."

She thinks a moment and then sits in the rocker by my door. The one my grandpap made by hand from an old hickory tree. She crosses her legs at the knees like Mr. Buster. Not at the ankles, like Jonah's mother. "Yes. Like you, Miss Octobia May. Now off to sleep."

9

A NEW FRIEND FOR BOTH OF US

Running barefooted on the cobblestones, I hop, skip, and take one giant leap over horse droppings in the street. "Hi, Mr. Sam." I stop. Just for a second. To pat Johnny's wet nose. "Good horse." I look into Mr. Sam's blue eyes to see if it's okay to grab a carrot stick from his vegetable wagon and feed it to Johnny. He neighs while he eats. Then I go on my way.

I'm supposed to be on punishment, but Auntie set it back by a day. When she saw the truck piled sky high with furniture, she changed her own rules. Now there's an apple pie cooling on the window ledge for our new neighbors. Lard melting in the iron skillet on the stove. Chicken plucked clean, ready for frying.

"Hi. My name is Octobia May. Excuse my bare feet. I was in Auntie's garden picking tomatoes. Checking on the onions and such. Do you eat onions?" I sit beside her on the red sofa resting on the pavement. "I do not like them. Radishes. I like them best. I know your name. Bessie." I am talking plenty. Maybe too much, Auntie would say. But I am too excited to slow down.

Bessie is as quiet as a Sunday afternoon. Wearing white gloves, a pleated white skirt and top, plus white patent leather shoes, she looks like an angel. And stares a lot. I do, too. At her Negro mother and white father. And then at Bessie, with long black hair, with nearly an ounce of Negro showing up on her skin.

I think up more things to say. "I know all about your family." I talk about the newspaper article. "Your mother's having a baby. Auntie says our whole country is in a family way — Negroes and whites alike. Good times, she says. People can see it coming like the light of a train miles back." I stop. To catch my breath. "So they have babies . . . lots and lots . . . sowing into tomorrow."

Bessie unsnaps her purse and stares inside.

"That's what Auntie says . . . anyhow."

Bessie is taller than me by a hair. I see that when she walks away, hugging her father like she's no plans to let go. He takes her by the hand. Walks her back to the sofa and says she must stay put while they work. Before he leaves he introduces himself to me. His name is Mr. Amadeo. "And that's Mrs. Amadeo. And, well, Bessie's a quiet girl. Not too many friends. Maybe you can come back later, okay?"

I wanted to talk about school. To ask if he knows the shortcut to get there. But he doesn't seem so friendly. Bessie, either. But her mother does. She takes me by the hand and says I should feel free to stay a spell.

She kisses her husband on the cheek. He pulls off his cap. She takes Bessie by the hand and leads us over to the couch. Scratching his wet forehead, her husband helps the men unload more furniture. Red kitchen chairs — with a matching red tabletop. A snow-white canopy bed. Yellow lamps with fancy fringes that dance when they move. And a pink vanity, Bessie's size. All things I sometimes see at Silverman's.

I ask Bessie if she wants to tour our neighborhood. Her mother answers yes. I ask if she always talks for Bessie. Her father answers this time. Maybe it's time for me to go home, he says, politely. "Bessie gets tired easily."

He walks into the house carrying a box marked *Fragile*. Dishes. His wife picks up a yellow mixing bowl and walks in behind him.

I ask Bessie about her voice. I knew a mute once. He was born not able to hear, either. "Did that happen to you, Bessie?"

She frowns.

I stare at my feet. What else can I do? Go home and begin my punishment? It's more fun to stay here and try to be neighborly. "Juppie!" I pick up my cat and watch her hop onto Bessie's lap. She stares at her, patting softly.

I watch the mud caked between my toes drying and cracking in the sun. And the men from the Ace moving van stepping off the truck again. That's when I see it. A real, for goodness' sake TV — an RCA Victor tabletop — and rabbit ears for good reception.

Lucy had a baby and they showed him on TV, I mention. "Have you seen him, Bessie? Little Ricky is his name." I love Lucy. And Ricky, her husband.

Bessie stares at me, smiling for the first time. I talk and talk about my favorite episodes. And Auntie, who I love, but who thinks that money should be in the bank, not tied up in things that land in the city dump. "I would never throw a television away." I want to follow theirs inside and sit and be with it all day. Even when all the shows end and the test pattern comes on. I would just stare at it all night long.

Juppie lays on the couch, yawning. Bessie stays as quiet as the yellow rose stuck in her hair. I think about Lucy and her best friend, Ethel. And wonder if Bessie and I will get to be good friends.

Her mother runs across the porch. "Mr. Amadeo says she can go." She is out of breath. "But please . . .

don't go too far. Or stay too long." Her eyes are on their front door. "He likes to be extra careful with her." She explains things to Bessie. And a few things to me. "Twenty minutes. It's all you have. Then he'll come looking. It's a new start, Bessie. For all of us."

I am ready to go, when a question lands in my head. "Sometimes, do people mistake Bessie for white?"

It takes her a minute to answer, so at first I think I am in trouble. It happens, she says, but they correct that. She is a proud Italian and a proud Negro, not one or the other.

"Sometimes people pass. Auntie told me that." They are Negro and pretend to be white.

"Bessie never will. We'll make sure of that." She asks me to keep ahold of Bessie's hand. I say I will. But I don't think it's right. She's ten. Like me. You can't hold on to us for too long.

When we get back around the corner, I let her hand go free. Stepping up to the fence, I look inside the graveyard. "I have lots of friends who don't talk." I'm thinking about the Before Girls and my pretend servant friends. "So if you never said a mumbling word, it would be okay with me."

I reach for her two hands and hold them up high so they face my hands.

I clap.

She claps.

I touch my left hand to her right hand. Then my right hand to her left one, and I start singing. "Miss Mary Mack, Mack, Mack, all dressed in black, black, black, with silver buttons, buttons, buttons, all down her back, back, back."

Bessie hangs on to her words, but her hands talk plain enough. Moving faster and faster, they keep up with my hands, along with the words in the song that keep speeding up, too.

Once we are done, I show her some of the neighborhood. Never mentioning you-know-who. I think she may be frightened of him. Of lots of things. But not of Juppie; she keeps her eyes on him. Even picking him up once.

When we get to her house, her father is pleased. "Three and a half minutes early. Great." He double-checks his Timex watch. "I like that Octobia May. A girl who keeps her word."

When I am on my steps looking across the street, I notice Bessie. Staring my way. Petting Juppie. Who also found a new friend today.

10

MAKING DEALS WITH JONAH'S MOTHER

Holding the heavy bucket with both hands, I walk across the porch stiff as Frankenstein. Our boarders sit rocking and fanning away the heat. "Excuse me." Kneeling down, I scrub under their feet and rockers. "Pardon me." I take my brush and spell my name on the floorboards in capital letters.

Auntie offers up lemonade and molasses cookies to Mrs. Ruby and the rest. I dunk the scrub brush into the water again. They laugh at Mr. Buster's jokes. I push my sour, sweaty bangs out of my eyes. Touching my hair with my shriveled up fingers, I think about the girls in *Jet* magazine. No tangles or plaits. Just long, straight, beautiful hair. "Hair is as bothersome as a dress," I tell my pretend servant friends. "If I had my way . . ."

Auntie can hear as well as any vampire. This dress and scrubbing are my punishment, she tells me, for traipsing around in the dead of the night chasing poor old Mr. Davenport. So she tells me to settle my mind and get back to work.

"Shuma." Jonah's mother walks up to our house, stomping across my clean porch. Jonah stands at the curb wearing a big smile. "I'd like to discuss your niece and something else of importance." Mrs. Nicholson drinks buttermilk for breakfast, I bet. She always looks as if she's had something sour. "Keep your distance, Jonah" — she points — "away from her."

Jonah squats behind a bush near the curb. His mother takes off her beige gloves, one finger at a time. "Morning, all," she says, beating Auntie into our house. "Fine day, ain't it?"

No sooner than the screen door slams shut, Jonah pops up. "Octobia May. I need you — quick." He holds out his hand, showing off his winnings. A handful of nickels. "I won. I did. I got more kisses than anybody else. Thanks." He promises to buy me anything I would like.

I don't want money. Or lemon cookies. I want to know if Jonah remembers that Mr. Davenport is a vampire, I say, looking at him from the porch. His crooked eye sets itself on me a good long time. "Jeepers creepers, Octobia May. You know I don't believe in vampires."

Walking down the steps, I set my bucket down and remind him again about Mr. Davenport's fangs. "Sorry, Octobia May. I didn't see his fangs."

I push back my hair and get down on my knees to scrub the pavement. Talking to my pretend servant friends, I ask why our lives are so hard and troubled. Jonah asks about my hair. He sniffs and picks at it like he's pulling weeds from the ground.

"Ouch!"

"Dresses and knotty hair," I say to my servant friends. "Boys do not know a thing about those."

Putting away his nickels, Jonah picks raspberries from our bush to eat. "Who's that?" he says when Bessie comes outside and sits on her front steps. Using his back pockets for a napkin, he wipes his hands clean.

"Bessie. The new girl." Juppie hears Bessie's name and walks across the street.

"Sure is pretty." Jonah fills his hands and mouth with more berries. Bessie sets her purse on the step, and picks up a comic book. Veronica from the Archie series. I can see them on the cover.

"She can't talk."

Juppie jumps in across her lap. "Guess you talk enough for the whole block, Octobia May." Jonah compliments her hair, asking when I last washed mine.

When our screen door squeaks open, all the rocking chairs stop. By the time Auntie and Jonah's mother step outside, he and I are back where we belong. I am on the pavement on my knees. Out of breath. Jonah is in the bushes.

"More freedom's coming than girls, or us coloreds, ever seen before." Auntie offers his mother a glass of cold tea. "A gal without a thimbleful of courage and wit will never make the best of it."

Jonah's mother huffs and puffs down the steps. She says that I do not have courage. I have a wild streak as long as Bend River. A reckless spirit that does not serve our neighborhood well. She frowns at my hair. She's a hairdresser and wonders when Auntie last took a hot comb to it.

I stand straight and tall and say I love my hair. She calls me haughty and proud.

"It's a poor frog that doesn't praise its own pond," Auntie says. Then she sets her hands on her hips. "Anyhow. You came for two things, Sarah Jean. Insulting my niece won't get your niece what you want."

I braid a loose plait while Mrs. Nicholson talks about her spinster niece. She is almost twenty-eight. The family wants her married. Jonah's mother stares up at Mr. Davenport's window. "Poor thing. He works so hard. No wonder he don't have the wherewithal to eat or mingle." She pats her pearl necklace.

"Vampires don't need food," I remind her.

Auntie gives me a good looking at. "Hush," she says out the side of her mouth.

Looking proud of herself, Mrs. Nicholson speaks louder than she needs to. "Every man needs a wife." Cutting her eyes at Auntie, she grunts. "Suitable Negro men to marry are a dime a dozen, if a woman does the necessary work to snag one."

Who would want their blood relations to marry a vampire? I think.

"Write the invitation. I'll pass it along to him," Auntie tells her.

"What invitation?" I'd like to know.

Auntie ignores me. "And I get in that group. Right?" She stops Mrs. Nicholson from trying to speak. "And these kids" — her finger points at me and Jonah still behind the bush — "they get to be children. Play together. Make mistakes. You agree?"

Mrs. Nicholson warns me. "Do not bring trouble to my door ever again, Octobia May." She puffs her hair, and faces Auntie. "The ladies in the group are all married, you know."

"I know."

"You'll be the only single one."

Auntie says she's got her reasons for wanting to be in that group. Walking up the steps, she tells me about the lady in the Do Some Good Ladies Club who is married to the chauffeur for the president of S and L Bank. She read it in the newspaper and has been thinking how good it would be if he spoke to him on her behalf. All the times she has gone to banks for a loan, it has not worked. But this just might, she thinks.

11

A HAIRDRESSER IN
THE BASEMENT

Jonah is wearing Auntie's pink bibbed apron. And her gardening gloves. He looks funny. But I'm not laughing. He's all set to put a perm in my hair. I wouldn't want him mad at me when he does it.

"Can you put curlers in my hair when you finish?" I ask Jonah. Auntie usually rolls my hair in twisted pieces of torn brown paper bags to set my curls. Jonah's got his mother's rollers. Pink spongy ones that snap closed. I feel grown-up already.

The fallout shelter is the best place to be in this house if you do not want to be found. So that's where we are.

It's nothing special — a concrete room with walls thick and tall enough to keep radiation out if the Russians ever came for us. There's a radio, batteries, medicine, and enough food and water to help us stay safe until help comes.

He pushes my head down. "I mixed water in it. Is that okay?"

He found a jar of crème relaxer in the trash at his mother's shop. It was dry and cracked like the desert. "You had to add water. How else would you loosen it up?"

He parts my hair with a rat-tail comb. I try not to cry when he hits a curl that won't turn the tooth loose. It was his idea to perm my hair, because of how it looked and smelled yesterday. Besides, he is paying me back for helping him win, he told me.

"You're doing a good job," I say after a while. I can't see, but I can feel how careful he's being. Parting. Spreading the white crème on. Apologizing when his elbow knocks me in the cheek accidentally.

Jonah washed my hair beforehand. And scratched my scalp. "The crème gets warm fast, huh?" I say, crossing and uncrossing my legs.

He says it's supposed to. "How else you gonna make your hair straight so it will do like you want?"

I am sweating, fanning my head, and drinking up the rest of his ice tea by the time he's done. "How long do you think we have to keep it on?"

He drops the empty jar in the trash and tells me to quit asking questions and let him comb the perm through my hair.

Aunt Shuma is against perms. Our hair is just the way God meant for it to be, she likes to say — kinky, curly, beautiful. "So why do you use the hot comb on it?" I ask her that a lot. She never answers that question. So I am here with Jonah's hands on my head because of her. If I waited for Aunt Shuma to see what's right under her nose, vampires and hair that shrinks and kinks in the summer would be the end of me.

I bring up Mr. Davenport to keep my mind off of my hair. The other day he padlocked his door to keep me out. Auntie approves. And she isn't concerned about Jonah's cousin, either. I saw her slide the invitation under Mr. Davenport's door this morning. Later I tried my best to get it. I stuck gum on the end of a yardstick and slid it underneath the door. It didn't work.

Jonah looks over the shelves of food. "That girl on that ring talk to you anymore?"

"No. She disappeared with the ring. But I'll find her."

He opens a can of sardines, eating them with his fingers. And says the more he thinks about it, the more he believes his mom is right. An author would make a good prize for his cousin. He clacks his teeth. "Her teeth are doubly big. That's why she's not married."

Fanning my head, I leave the padded shelter. Walking

circles around the casket and furnace, I listen out for Auntie. Stopping, I look over the shelves of food she canned. Pickled okra. Strawberry jam. Peach wine. Jelly labeled for Christmas. Today I will pay Jonah in jam, not kisses. Four jars that Auntie will never miss. "You wouldn't let your cousin date a vampire, would you?"

He walks in eating pork and beans from a can. "My family do not believe in vampires, Octobia May."

I do not argue. "My head feels awfully hot," I tell him. Carrying the jams over to him, I feel red-hot heat move from the nape of my neck — the place that Auntie calls "the kitchen" — to my forehead down to my eyebrows like I was struck by lightning. Flames fire up my scalp. "Jonah. My head's on fire!"

He is licking his fingers, one at a time. "Octobia May. No such thing can happen, and you know it."

Jars of jam and jelly burst open on the floor when I drop them. They turn his white socks pink and sprinkle his green shirt with blueberries. "Octobia May. My mother will . . ."

It feels like somebody threw gasoline on my head and lit a match. Running around the basement barefooted. Hopping over broken glass. I fan myself like it's August in Arkansas, where my cousin's church windows are rusted shut and the fans are always broken. "My head. My brain. I'm dying!"

Jonah comes over with the bottle of Argo spray

starch Aunt Shuma uses for her clothes. "Be still." He sprays my head, especially the edges and kitchen. He says that if I am a vampire killer it seems to him I could get my hair did without crying like a girl.

When my heart gave out the last time, I never cried after the doctors fixed and stitched it up. So after a few minutes I set my mind on ignoring my scalp. Even though it's burning so bad I want to call the fire department.

12

HAIR TODAY, GONE TOMORROW

Jonah comes up with something he thinks will keep my mind busy. Playing catch. We are using a baseball signed by Satchel Paige, but not really signed by him. It's Jonah's signature. Temporarily. Until he runs across the real Mr. Paige and gets his.

After a while, Jonah brings up Mr. Davenport and his cousin. Next week he will come to their house for a light supper. "Look." The note Mr. Davenport sent Jonah's mother is wrinkled and folded when Jonah pulls it out of his pocket. "He is a writer. See, he typed it."

I roll my fingers over the black letters.

Dear Mrs. Nicholson, the note begins.

Please know that it is my honor and distinct pleasure to dine with you and your lovely niece. As an author, however, my hours are not in accordance with most others' in the world. While you serve your employer or tend to your fine family, I rest from a long, challenging night of putting ink to paper. It has always been so, since I was in my youth. So it continues. If it is not presumptuous of me, I would love to meet your family. Then take a walk by the river with your beautiful niece, Geraldine. Writing is such a solitary activity. Authors do not tend to do well in crowds of two or more. Bold and brazen are we on clean white paper. Dull as a napping pup in another's company. I do hope your niece will not be finished with me after a second or so. I do tend to be shy, even ignoring the other boarders in our quaint home. Oh, I've not a mean bone in my body, but a quiet spirit so few seem to understand. Oh, the stories I've heard about myself. More imaginative than I could spin in a thousand years. But please know this: I am a gentleman. I do not go where I am not invited. And a late evening supper, after the sun sets, works for me best.

Yours truly,
Hardy Davenport VIII

I am reading the note for the third time when Jonah says how excited his whole family is. His mother is planning a candlelit meal on the back porch. "Like they do in the movies." Everyone is excited. Other neighbors on his block have seen the note and plan to surprise Mr. Davenport with a visit after they eat. They have never met a real live author before. And they want to hear his stories about the war.

Jonah smacks the letter on his leg. "There you see, Octobia May. Why nobody believes you? His letter is proof he is who he say he is. A writer. A good one, too."

Mr. Davenport's words are the most beautiful I've ever read. Elegant. And nobody can say any different.

Jonah leads me over to the sink, not far from the casket. "Just maybe he is what he say he is. A fine, upstanding Negro writer that don't care for people much, Octobia May — especially girls who tell such whoppers."

I don't say a word. My head is hurting. My scalp is burning. I do not want to scream, but . . . "Water! Jonah. Please." I help him turn on the faucet. "Ohhhh. Ahhhh . . ." His hands feel like angel wings when they pat my head.

Watching the crème go down the drain, I look for blood. Because it feels like that crème did more than make my hair straight.

"Hey." Jonah quits rubbing shampoo onto my scalp.

"Look." He's waving a baby ponytail. "I guess some-times a little hair come out, huh?"

The more Jonah rubs, the more hair falls out. It's lying in the tub like corn silk, clogging up the drain. Water and suds and crème spin around while the cool, cold water runs over my hot scalp.

Jonah pats my arm.

"Get me a mirror."

He doesn't want to.

"I need to see."

He sneaks up the stairs and comes back with the smallest mirror in the house. I think he did it on pur-pose, just so I wouldn't see how bad I look. "Go get Aunt Shuma," I say, without screaming or crying. I'm remembering what my sisters say about me always being strong. I died once before, didn't I? I came back, too. The doctors say I am the bravest little girl they've ever seen.

Sitting up, I watch my hair falling out without my even touching it. We got it straight, though — there's not one curl or kink in it.

13

THE BOY IN THE MIRROR

Before I died I was not afraid of everything. Even boys. Even letting my father pull out my loose front tooth. Once you pass, you come back different. "Go ahead," I tell Aunt Shuma. "Finish. It won't bother me any."

Aunt Shuma cuts off the rest of my hair, slow and sorrowful, like she is cutting her best friend's obituary out the newspaper. Stepping back, she sets down the shears. "A bald head is not pretty, Octobia May. You'll regret —"

"It's my hair."

"And wait till I find that Jonah." Auntie snaps the scissors open and closed. "I'd like to give him a haircut, I would."

Mr. Buster hands her a can of Barbasol shaving cream. Foaming up her fingers, Auntie rubs it over my scalp. Then slides the straight razor across my head over and over again. "If you tell your parents, I will be disowned." Staring at my head, she makes it plain. "Lordy, what a mess."

Mr. Buster hands me an empty Florsheim shoe box. "Bury your hair right away," he says, smoothing back his conked hair. "Leave it sitting around," he says, "and anything can happen to you and it. Birds build nests with it and you end up with a headache. People who don't like you use it to ruin your good night sleep." Auntie said he could leave the room if all he could do was add to my troubles.

I do not need to look at myself in the mirror. I can tell how I look by watching their faces. Mrs. Ruby comes into the kitchen, pointing her cane at me. "Ringworm. What a pity."

Auntie kisses her, then says it is better to tell people I slept at a friend's house and caught ringworm than to tell them I was foolish enough to let a boy perm my hair. "I'd rather be pitied than scorned," she tells me.

I walk my hair box to the garden and almost bury it there. But then I see *him* standing in the window staring down at me. I take out my garlic. Peel and chew it. And finger the letter Jonah passed along to me. It's a vampire trick that will get his cousin killed. I know it.

I am nearly at the corner when I hear it. Footsteps. Following me.

I pick up Juppie, to make a run for it. "Bessie?"

She stares. I take her hand. "I could use a friend today," I say, walking her into the graveyard. Sitting underneath my favorite tree, I ask it to take good care of my treasure. And we both take turns digging up the ground with Auntie's favorite spoon.

"Hey. You, boy. What you doing over there? Oh. Octobia May." The gravediggers know me by name. Standing, holding pitchforks and shovels, they ask what has become of my hair.

I pat my smooth scalp. "I like it this way for summer."

Staring at Bessie, the tallest one stabs the ground with his shovel. "A bald-headed gal. I seen everything now."

Bessie and I keep walking. I do not hold her hand. I let her carry Juppie. She smiles a lot when she does.

When we get to the Before Girls, I ask if they ever had to part with their hair. Of course they never answer. I pull up weeds around their grave. Bessie sits and stares.

When I get to the Jewish section, I stop. Picking up a tiny stone, I sit it on a grave next to a pile of other stones. It's tradition. A sign of respect. The stones tell everyone that people still care about you, I tell Bessie. When I go to visit my other friends, Bessie takes herself home. Juppie lays down beside me after a while. Before I know anything, we are both asleep.

"Young man. Wake up. Where is your mother?"

I sit up, rubbing my eyes. The graveyard manager pulls me up by my left ear. "Boy, why are you here disturbing my people?"

"Mr. Alexander. It's me. Octobia May."

He stands back, rubbing his pointy chin. Patting his belly, he burps. "Patched overalls. And now a bald head. No wonder I had mistaken you for a boy." Taking me by the arm, he reminds me how often he's warned me to stay out. "I've said it to you time and time again, Octobia May. People do not wish to hear you talking to the dead."

"But I . . ."

He marches me past the gravediggers and through Peaceful Grove and Everlasting Lane. He stops to yank up a ripped, faded flag waving over a grave. It reminds me of those other soldier flags. I wonder if they are still there.

Inside the main building, Mr. Alexander sits at his roll-top desk. His cauliflower ears have gray hair crawling out of them. Little blond hair sits on his chin. "Sit," he says, picking up and putting down papers on his busy desk. While he writes, I ask about Mr. Davenport. I meant to all along. "Does he really work here?" I tell him about the mausoleum and the ring, before I ask if he believes in vampires.

"Silence." Mr. Alexander writes faster. "And do not pester me with your nonsensical questions again." When he finishes, he reads me every word.

Dear Miss Shuma,

I have said it before. I will say it once more. Your niece Octobia May is not welcome at my cemetery. If the deceased need plants or the Mayor Schakowsky statue needs to be repaired up, one of my men shall be happy to do so. By the way, I do not pay my grounds-keepers to drink Octobia May's strawberry lemonade or have her fan their sweat away. Therefore, this very day, I am instructing Officer O'Malley to keep your niece out of my facility. These are harsh measures, but what else can I do? A child does not belong in a graveyard. And the dead are not her playmates!

Eternally yours,
Albert Alexander

Mr. Alexander slides the note into a long beige envelope. I am apologizing for upsetting him. It's not that he dislikes me, he says, "But you simply go too far, young lady."

On my way out his office, I see a bald-headed boy in

the mirror. "Is that me?" I do not mean to speak the words out loud, but I surprised myself.

"It's a shocker," Mr. Alexander says, putting his hand on my left shoulder, "but no surprise." He walks me to the back door, complaining. A few minutes later, he brings up my parents even though he's never met them. "Educated, good, decent people. It's clear to see. I'm certain they would never approve of the way your aunt is rearing you." He stays by my side until I am outside the gate. And even though closing time is hours away, he locks the gate behind me.

14

A STAKE FOR MR. DAVENPORT

I think Auntie told everyone to pretend not to notice my head, because when I get home that is what they all do. Pretend.

"Hello, Octobia May. Certainly a nice day we're having, isn't it?" Mrs. Ruby has cataracts, but her eyes follow my head like a searchlight.

Mr. Piers sits at the organ, running his fingers over the keys. "Octobia May. Would you like a lesson? I'm ready. And today it's free."

I sit down beside him. For two hours, we practice "Unforgettable," a song by Mr. Nat King Cole. And other songs that sound better on a piano.

Feeling the keys is like touching my scalp. Smooth. I make lots of mistakes. And wonder. Is good and evil like piano or organ keys? Sitting side by side. Making it easy for people to mistake one for the other.

Mrs. Loewenthal comes into the room wearing a wide smile on her face. Asking if I'd like to play gin rummy. It's Jonah who rescues me. Walking into our house, Jonah sets a brown bag on my lap — with a wig inside. "To cover my mistake, Octobia May."

I hurry him outside. Explaining that I do not want a wig. But I could use his help, following Mr. Davenport wherever he goes on Sunday. I thought it up on the way home from the graveyard. If Jonah goes, we will be even Steven. "And get to save your cousin, too."

Jonah folds the bag over and frets. He is in his mother's good graces, these days. And wants to stay that way, he says. But he is a good friend and cousin. So he agrees to meet me here tomorrow night. But only after I ask how he would feel if his cousin got bit and turned all his relatives into red-eyed, blood-sucking vampires.

I look over the railing into the bushes, hoping no one will ever find the letter I hid in there. Then off to the wooden shed we go, pulling out an old bicycle Auntie saved from the rubbish pile. He follows me up and down the block and around the corner when I ride. I do the same for him. Until I see Mr. Buster. His yellow tie matches his yellow shoes, which make his short, skinny feet look like bananas.

Leaving my bike on the pavement, I follow Mr. Buster up our porch steps. "Why you dressed up?"

"Just interviewed. Start tomorrow. First thing. Thank God people still dying."

Jonah stands on the pavement eating raspberries. "What they gonna have you doing, Mr. Buster?"

He looks up and down the street like he has a secret to tell us. "I'll be dressing the bodies."

Jonah frowns. "Putting on shoes and pants and slips?"

"Boxers, too?" I want to know.

He doesn't know all the particulars, he says. "Gonna do what they tell me, even if it means putting wigs on heads or cutting toenails with my teeth."

Jonah ducks when Auntie finds her way to the sitting room window. Sitting on the sofa, she talks to us through the screen. She asks Mr. Buster if this is what will happen, him talking work at night while we eat. Telling us what color socks the man around the corner wore into the grave.

He thinks everything she says is funny, so he laughs. "I am a man who is used to working, day and night." He picks up Juppie, who is trying to get to me. "So even if I have to be the box they lay the body in, I'll do it. Work is good for the soul."

He ignores me for a while and only talks to Auntie. Jonah stays hidden behind the bushes. When Mr. Buster asks Auntie to the movies, she blushes when she says she couldn't possibly. Then she heads for the kitchen.

Mr. Buster pinches my nose. "'Case nobody said it. Your crown and glory look beautiful to me."

I pat my head. "For a minute," I say, hugging my knees, "I forgot I didn't have any hair." Sitting closer to him, I whisper, "Do you know where I can buy a stake, Mr. Buster?"

Laughing, Mr. Buster says, "Well, I do not."

Jonah heads across the street to Bessie's house. Juppie follows behind him with her head up high. When Bessie's father walks onto the porch, he waves her inside. Stopping, he stares at me a while before he goes in the house.

Maybe it's the disappointment on my face that makes Mr. Buster stand up. "But follow me." His yellow shoes tap the steps and walk over the grass Auntie mows every other Thursday. And into our rigidity wooden shed.

I am thinking about Mr. Davenport when I say, "Stakes are the only true way to kill a vampire."

Mr. Buster picks over rusty nails and hammers. A broken axhammer and lightbulb. "Can't say if you right about how to handle vampires. But just in case I need you to save me from one — colored or not — I'll lend you this." He laughs when he taking a broken flat-tip screw-driver out of his toolbox. I walk back to the house with it tucked in my socks. "A vampire killer sleeping right upstairs from me," he says. "I feel safer already."

Auntie is on the porch when we get back. Leaning over the railing, she calls for Jonah, who is now march-ing up the street like a soldier. The fishing rod he carries on his shoulder is the rifle he's taking to war, he tells Auntie. "To kill those communists."

Henry is walking beside him, not Bessie. "No," Henry says. "We're playing cowboys and Indians." He aims a pole at me. "Pow." Laughing, he says, "Look. I scalped her."

Jonah and Henry march up our cobblestone street. Auntie looks me over, staring extra long at my head. Mr. Buster winks at her and goes inside. "Jonah. I need to talk to you."

"It's only hair," I tell Auntie. "It'll grow back." I begged her not to tell Jonah's mother what he did to my hair the other day. I wanted him to perm it. Besides, there's nothing his mother can do to him that will bring my hair back. I say this again to Auntie, squeezing her tight around the middle. Reminding her about the time she wanted the wind to catch her.

She rubs my bald head. "Children just plain foolish."

By the time Jonah sets foot on our pavement, Auntie has changed her mind. She tells him to get along to his fishing and to bring her back a few catfish if he comes across them. He smiles. "Look, Octobia May. My winnings bought me friends." Running after Henry, he says for him to wait up. Not that Henry does.

Auntie walks into the house and comes back with a baby brush and a cup of olive oil sprinkled with jasmine grown in our yard. Oiling my scalp, she sings the song my mother sang to me when I was sick in the hospital right after I was born — and then two years ago.

I was born with my heart outside of my chest. The doctors put it back in the right place, but every once in a while it gives me trouble. "Your heart quit beating twice that last time," Aunt Shuma reminds me. "For ten minutes," we both say.

The doctors say that it isn't possible, but I heard my family singing while I was dead. Their song snuck up the hall and opened the operating room door. It leaked into the anesthesia, dripping into me like new blood. When I woke up from being dead, I was singing that song.

15

A WHISTLING WOMAN

The best day of the week for evil to do its business is Sunday. The churches are full. And their doors are shut. We have blue laws. You're not allowed to sell anything, so not one store is open. After worship, people stay inside with family. Or go to bed early. There's nothing to stop bad from doing whatever it wants. Even policemen can't hardly be found.

"Hurry, Jonah." I rush around the corner, peeking across the street at Mr. Davenport. He is walking past the graveyard, whistling his way up the street.

Vampires can hear tomorrow coming. So you have to be quiet as a flea, if you're following them. I am wearing black socks. No shoes. Walking on my toes when I can. Jonah wore brand-new Buster Brown shoes. Already they hurt his feet. "Oh, Octobia May . . ."

"Shush. He'll hear you."

". . . My feet." He sits in the middle of the pavement, untying brown laces. Pulling off his socks and shoes, he wiggles and rubs his toes.

I pat my right pocket. It's filled with baby crosses made from the funny papers. I pull up my pant leg to check the screwdriver I brought along. When Mr. Davenport stops at the graveyard gate, I hold my breath. But just as I thought, he keeps walking.

Juppie prances up to me, meowing. "Quiet. Scat. Go home." Shooing her along doesn't help. She sits like the stone lions at the cemetery gate. I give her a good, stern looking at, and finally she heads back home. I follow Mr. Davenport on my own.

He is a good citizen when it doesn't matter much. He waits to cross on green even with no cars coming. He tips his hat at ladies passing by. His black Stacy Adams shoes, quiet as the synagogue they stand in front of, point toward Bend River across the street. People throw things in there. So that river knows all the secrets people be trying to hide, I think. Like who killed Mr. Mars.

Mr. Davenport walks over to the river and drops something in. "The ring." I cover my mouth. He drowned it, I think. I think about the girl on the ring, and feel sad.

Jonah catches up to me, out of breath. His knotted shoestrings hold his shoes snug over his shoulder. "What — what . . . if he don't bite nobody tonight, Octobia May? Then my momma's gonna whip me for nothing."

I squeeze my fingers deep down into my pocket, past a lucky string and a rabbit's foot. "You'll still win this." I open my hand wide.

Jonah plucks the nickel out of my palm. "I like to win, Octobia May. I truly do."

I'll let Jonah keep the nickel. It will encourage him to want to find out the truth about Mr. Davenport. "But quit blabbering. Or we will be his supper."

Standing in a shadow. Quiet as the moon. We listen to the water patting the rocks. A nice couple walks by the river. Holding hands, they stop and look across it.

Jonah whispers. "What's it like to live with white people? Like them. Octobia May."

"I don't know."

"Sure you do. Mrs. Loewenthal's white."

"She's Jewish."

"Ain't it the same?"

"Auntie says no."

"Can a person be a Negro and a Jew, Octobia May?"

"I guess if they have colored vampires, they can surely have Negro Jews," I say to him, watching the couple move on.

We pass the hat factory, the icehouse, and Dave's Dairy, which delivers the sweetest bottled milk in the city. Jonah brings up Bessie's father. "Italians are white, right?"

"They look it," I say, wishing he would stop questioning me. Then I think about Bessie. And wonder, *Who makes up the rules about what people is and ain't, anyway?*

Mr. Davenport walks. And walks. Until his feet find streets where people and the moon try never to go. A woman in tall red heels walks up the block by herself. Strolling along, she swings a clutch purse. Mr. Davenport steps aside at first. Then follows her.

Death does not look like people think it should. Sometimes it wears summer suits and fine hats, silk gloves, and handmade shoes. Like him.

In the hospital I was bloody and cut up, but even when I died they said I was smiling. Is he smiling? Is that why she stops and speaks to him? Can't she smell trouble? Even a kitten knows when a skunk is close by.

Hiding underneath a weeping willow tree, Jonah and I keep watch. Sweat runs off my bald head, rolling behind my ears and down my neck. Those two do not look bothered by the heat at all. They look like friends.

The woman is dressed in all white, like a bride. But her red lips look bloody under the streetlight. She stands straight and tall, her hair curled tight, not afraid of the heat. Jonah tries to step out from under the trees, but I make him stay put. He spits. "Gnats, Octobia May, is getting in my mouth."

In his ear, I whisper, "Don't you want to save somebody, Jonah? Keep evil from having its way?" I mention his cousin. Only Jonah and I can save her. This lady, too.

He smiles. And agrees. "She does not have a husband, Octobia May. She needs a boy like me protecting her, huh?"

"Yes, Jonah. Now quiet."

Jonah and I are spies, ducking between a white Chevrolet and a green Plymouth with thick whitewall tires and silver teeth. Walking swiftly up streets, we try to stay in the shadows. Crossing against the light, Mr. Davenport and the lady keep their backs to us. She takes his arm, rushing and whistling along the way. Whistling.

16

PROOF

We crawl underneath porches. Stand in mud. Hide
behind light poles. And, holding hands, we make the
same turns they make. "No," I whisper, when they get
to Clinton Avenue. "Don't let him take you there."

They had a big fire on Clinton Avenue, a very long
time ago. It went from house to house like polio, taking
people's lives and making folks leave their homes, Aunt
Shuma told me once. She gave me my instructions soon
as I moved in. "Don't go on Clinton. Some of them
dead folks still cry about what happened to 'em."

Maybe the lady in white never heard the story. Or
maybe she likes how he holds her by the elbow and

stares into her eyes. I guess that's why she starts to walk up Clinton like it's broad daylight and a picnic lunch is waiting for her.

I cover my mouth when she passes the first two houses. My eyes squint by the time they get to the middle of the block. I never saw anyone die before.

Jonah wants to go home. I share a piece of my garlic with Jonah. "My mother was wrong about him. He would kill my cousin. I know it." He looks up and down Clinton Avenue. It's a dead-end street, with boarded-up houses and empty lots. The streetlamp at the opposite end of the block flickers. The one across from us isn't working at all. Gnats in the tree we are standing underneath join their cousins on my scalp.

Mr. Davenport and the lady in white talk like old friends. She is happy to see him again. Is he better, she wants to know. Able to sleep "a tad" at night? He takes his hat off and lets out a long breath. He never sleeps, he says. He thinks he never will again. She squeezes his arm and mentions the war. His voice turns into a sharp nail. "Let's not discuss that. You know the real reason I'm here."

She walks by four houses, too far away for me to hear. Jonah's feet are spikes dug deep in the ground, when I try to pull him along.

I strain. But I can hear a few words. Like *bank*, *passing*, and *money*. I think they are talking about passing stolen money. But to who? And who stole it? *Mr. Davenport?* I wonder. Not the lady. She looks so pretty.

I leave Jonah when they start walking. And I tiptoe to another tree. Then I hide in the shadows of one of the houses. Crossing an empty lot, I get closer than ever before. Someone double-crossed Mr. Davenport, I learn. Or maybe he double-crossed them. His voice lowers after he mentions Bend River.

The lady is nervous. Raising her voice, until he tells her to quiet down. She points. "That's the house. Seven thirty-nine. Empty now. It's under the kitchen floorboards. Where he hid it. Now where's my mon —"

Mr. Davenport holds on to her wrist and tries to pull her along. Using her purse like a hammer, she hits him. And hits him some more. His hand is high in the air when she says, "Don't. My husband . . . I'm leaving town tonight."

He holds on to her wrist, pulls her toward the street.

The lady loses a shoe, trying to stay where she is. "Please." She doesn't scream or whisper. She begs. "Randy . . . My husband . . . I gave it to him. You know that. He made the decisions . . . I'm sorry." Another shoe comes off and her legs buckle. "Keep the money. Let me go."

Mr. Davenport drags her along.

A porch light comes on. The lady and Mr. Davenport

are as still as the wheels of the car behind them. Me too. Until she runs, screaming. "Help. He'll kill me."

The bulb on the porch goes off.

Mr. Davenport chases the lady. I run to Jonah. "Go home. Run. Get help," I whisper.

"Octobia May. Don't you die." Jonah's feet smack the pavement. His shoes fall from his shoulders when he turns the corner and disappears.

No sooner than Jonah leaves Clinton Avenue, Mr. Davenport turns into his real, true self. Pulling the lady up the street. He covers her mouth with his hand. The streetlamp only shines so far. So even with them under it, I can only see a little. The way he is whispering in her ear and turning her neck. How she stops moving. Legs and arms limp as Raggedy Ann's.

I close my eyes when his hands hold her throat and he leans over her.

Blood. I see it, I do. On his lips and jacket, when he is passing by my hiding tree. Red as her lips.

He stops to wipe his shoes with the monogrammed handkerchief Auntie ironed yesterday. Dirt, not the dead lady he left behind, is what bothers him.

I raise my stake.

"Octobia May!" His hands, heavy and strong as the steel my uncle Rio makes at the mill in Pittsburgh, weigh down my arm. I drop the screwdriver.

"Please don't kill me."

He laughs. "Look at the sun begging the night for one more day."

My teeth chatter and my knees knock.

"Meow."

"Juppie!"

Hissing, she bites and scratches at his legs. He pulls up his pant legs to check for blood. When he stands — Juppie claws his chin. And turns him meaner than a hound dog at a hunt. Lifting her by the fur on her back, he throws her. When her head hits the hubcap of a car, I scream.

Mr. Davenport strolls back over to the dead lady. The neighbors keep their doors shut and their lights off. Picking up Juppie, I run home.

17

JONAH'S MOTHER AND THE LAW

Fire engines pass me by. Sirens scream the news: Clinton Avenue is in trouble again. "They'll see Juppie. I was right all the time."

Once I get in the house, Auntie and the rest smother me with hugs and kisses. Jonah pushes his way over to me, too. "He bit her. Didn't he?" His hands fly this way and that. "How 'bout the bite marks on her neck, Octobia May. Was they big?"

I am standing with my mouth wide open so long, breathing hard and catching my breath, that dribble rolls down my chin. Auntie wipes it away, shaking me.

"Octobia May. What's happening to you? Did somebody hurt you out there?"

"You — you saw him, Jonah. Didn't you? See, Auntie. I — I was telling the truth."

Before she can answer, Jonah's mother, Mrs. Nicholson, comes in from the kitchen. Her feet set Auntie's china-cabinet teacups to rattling. "Well, la-di-da." She frowns when she gets a good look at my head. "You and your vampire stories."

They all line up beside me — Auntie, Mr. Buster, Mrs. Ruby, Mrs. Loewenthal, Miss Marble, and Mr. Piers. Jonah and his mother are on the other side. "Are you all saying" — Mrs. Nicholson holds tight to her black leather purse — "that you support her wild tales?"

Auntie's hair is set in rag curlers, held tight to her head with a hairnet. She takes her time answering. "Octobia May know vampires are pretend. Jonah do, too." The pockets in her housedress get a working, with her shoving her hands in and out of them. "But they saw something. Don't you think?" She's pointing at Jonah. "He came here looking like death was riding him. That's why I sent for you."

Mrs. Nicholson stoops to Jonah's height. "Yes he did. No thanks to her."

"Mom. He's a killer. A murderer." Jonah tries to get to me. His mother's hands hold him back. "He kidnapped someone."

"Juppie scratched him hard. Didn't she, Jonah?"

When Jonah says he wasn't there for that part, Auntie walks into another room and comes back with the castor oil and a tablespoon. Dressed in pajamas, wearing a plaid robe, Mr. Buster changes the subject to the police. "I called 'em. From the corner phone. May take 'em forever to get here."

Mrs. Loewenthal goes into the kitchen. Jonah wants to tell his story. He starts with his Buster Brown shoes. Walking over to him, I move the night along. "We went on Clinton Avenue. We saw him dragging the girl. His teeth broke open her neck. Skin and blood dropped onto his mouth and fingers. Jonah knows."

Jonah flips my nickel between one finger and the next. "Well, I didn't go up Clinton Avenue too far."

The grown-ups in the room stop like broken watches and stare at me. All except Mrs. Loewenthal. She walks around the room carrying a silver tray. "I made this coffee. Have a cup. Relax."

"Relax! You heard my boy. He never stepped a foot on that block. How he see Mr. Davenport hurt someone?"

Jonah tries to speak, but someone is knocking at our door. Officer O'Malley. "Octobia May, let the man in," Auntie says, looking at me differently now.

"Jesus, Mary, and Joseph. What has happened to your hair, girlie?"

"Mr. Davenport killed a lady tonight. Tell him, Jonah."

Jonah runs up to Officer O'Malley. "I ain't see it but —"

Rushing past me, Mrs. Nicholson's long, cool Sunday dress flies behind her. "She got my son believing nonsense." Her finger points to me.

"Sarah Jean. Do not point at the child." Auntie's voice is firm and steady. "Even a no-count bum on the street deserves not to be pointed at."

She puts her hand in her dress pocket. Mrs. Loewenthal pours coffee. Officer O'Malley and I get offered the very first cups. "This is what the problem is." Jonah's mother stands beside Officer O'Malley. "She get treated like a woman." She says I have more rights than all the Negroes in this city put together. "Officer O'Malley. Sir. Children in this city got curfews, don't they?" She stops Jonah when he breaks free and tries to sip from my cup.

"It's not a night to talk curfews, ma'am." Officer O'Malley is tall, with hair that doesn't like to stay put. He pats it every second he is with you. "We checked Clinton Street . . . Avenue . . . and did not find a body. Nor a drop of blood." He sits and stirs his coffee.

"Jonah. Boy. Did you see the vampire, or not?"

He is smiling, until Mrs. Nicholson mentions it. Then he gets as upset as she is. "I've had enough of your shenanigans." He jumps to his feet.

"What did you see, son?"

Jonah looks at me. "Octobia May. I seen him with that woman. I truly did. I heard her screaming." He looks at his mother. "Mr. Davenport ain't erase my memories this time." He looks at Officer O'Malley. "I woulda seen him bite her if I stuck around long enough."

I drink up my coffee. Juppie hops off my lap, goes into the kitchen and down the basement steps. Officer O'Malley scratches his head. Miss Marble has been sitting in the corner all this time, blowing her coffee. She likes it black without sugar. "Where he at, then? That devil. Are you going to question him, hard as you questioned this child?"

"I will not be asking a grown man if he bit someone tonight, lady." His eyes find mine. "Her imagination. Mrs. Nicholson is right. It's high time you tamed it, Shuma. This is a decent colored family you were born into, Octobia May; do you want your foolishness to give it a bad name?"

Mrs. Nicholson stands next to the officer. "You may as well accept it, Shuma. The girl is common. Plain and simple."

Common is what they call the girl around the corner who combs her hair on the front porch steps in broad daylight. *Common* is what they call Mrs. Edwards — who is really a Miss and living with someone else's husband. It is one of the worse things you can call a person.

I run out of the room, letting the teacup fall from my lap. Jonah would like to tag along. But his mother says she will spank him if he does. So he stays behind. "I believe you, Octobia May!" he shouts. "Even if my mother don't like it!"

Down the basement steps, turning as they go, I call for my pretend servant friends. No one answers. Looking around for Juppie, I think how much I wish she could talk. "Then you could tell them what you saw. And what happened to you." I walk over and sit on the crate Uncle Lester sent us. It was full of peaches from Maryland. With your nose to the wood, you can still smell his farm. Standing in the middle of the room, I look about for Juppie. Under the casket. Behind the basket of apples Auntie picked up from the store. Beside the furnace. I look everywhere for her. Even in the bomb shelter. "Come out, Juppie. Here, girl."

Auntie stands in the kitchen at the basement door. "Octobia May. Don't make me come down there, child. Get yourself up here."

"There you are. I thought you were hiding. You're tired. Asleep." Her legs peek out from under the washing machine. She naps there sometimes. I forgot.

Auntie says Officer O'Malley would like one last

word with me. So she wants me in the dining room lickety-split.

"Come on, girl, out. Juppie?" Poking her. Pulling her by her legs, I feel my heart speed up.

"Octobia May!" Auntie walks down the spiral stairs. "How many times —"

Holding Juppie in my arms, I rock and beg her to open her eyes. Auntie kneels down beside me, rubbing my back. "It's all my fault, girl. Death likes to follow me."

18

BROKEN THINGS

He killed my cat. All night long I held her, even though Auntie didn't approve. First thing this morning, I laid Juppie in a hatbox full of lemon peels, rubber bands, blueberries, and comic strips — things that gave her fun when she was alive.

I will bury her at the graveyard. Auntie's already gotten Mr. Alexander's permission. She figured he would be more agreeable if the asking didn't come from me. Even though I have been a disappointment to her lately, she says.

Kicking up his heels. Saluting me as good as any Russian soldier, Jonah walks down our steps. When we get to the corner, Bessie lines up behind him. She has a Brownie camera around her neck. Standing with her head held high, she looks like someone important is going into the ground.

We walk around the block one behind the other. Me with my arms wrapped around the hatbox as carefully as silk ribbons tied into bows. Jonah carries a rusty shovel. Bessie doesn't help dig or push dirt aside, once we find a spot. She watches. So does her camera. Taking a picture of Juppie's beautiful box, she is as quiet as the dead. Snapping her camera while Jonah digs, she hardly moves. *Click.* Bessie will tell what happened today. *Click.* Me crying. Jonah laying a white shoebox in the ground. Dirt falling off the shovel. Three Popsicle-stick crosses tied together with string. *Click.*

I hand Jonah and Bessie each a cross. All together at the same time we stick them deep in the sandy dirt over Juppie. Sitting three stones beside them, I ask God to walk her up to heaven.

We are almost out of the graveyard when we see Mr. Alexander at the gate. Putting a fresh wreath on the fence. *Click.* He sits wire and a hammer on the ground. Brushing his dusty hands on his pants, he says how sorry he is to learn about Juppie. "Any death is hard on the heart." But he warns me, no more visiting after today. I am thinking about the note when he brings it up. Did I pass it on to Auntie? He forgot to ask her about it. The day she came was a busy one. "Three funerals and a grandbaby on the way."

Jonah rescues me. Taking me and Bessie by the arm, he says I'm due to get hair tonic on my head at his mother's shop. Mr. Alexander eyes my head and shakes his own. Outside the graveyard, I pick up a stick. Tapping it along the cemetery fence, I make music. Mr. Alexander stops me. Jonah asks why I am forever in trouble. I toss the stick. Bessie stares. *Click.*

"That fellow, his name was what? Devonshire? Davenport?"

"Yes. Davenport."

"Never heard of him." Mr. Alexander lifts a spool of wire. My question from awhile ago about Mr. Davenport working for him got lost in his head, he says, and didn't show itself until he was all set for bed one night and found himself with a headache.

I dance up the street. Jonah asks why I'm so happy. Auntie will never believe in vampires. Or my stories, he thinks. I do not plan to cry, but I do. Jonah brushes away my tears. Juppie wouldn't want me crying, he says. "Besides, what if you chasing after vampires when something worse is living in your house?"

"Worse?"

"A killer, Octobia May. A plain old ordinary everyday regular murderer. Nothing special, like maybe you want." He picks up a stick, and makes his own music.

I scratch my head.

Bessie stops by the end of the fence. *Click.* She takes a picture of the soldiers' graves. The flags catch our attention again. Someone's replaced the old ones, even though they weren't that old. Staring at me, I see a tear in her eye. "Come on, Bessie. Let's get you home."

19

THE END OF THE ROAD FOR ME

As soon as Aunt Shuma and Mr. Buster turn the corner, Mr. Davenport steps onto the porch. Sitting in a rocker, he looks up at the sky. "The sun, I miss it."

I stare at the sun myself. Blinking, I say, "You're gonna die. The sun will kill you."

"Can't you tell? We colored vampires are nothing like all the rest." He smiles. "After some years, the sun becomes our friend. Not our enemy."

Patting my pockets, I back away from him. Then I remember. I don't have my garlic. I was crying over Juppie earlier, not worrying about Mr. Davenport. I begin to cry all over again when I talk to him about her. "You hurt her last night when you threw her. That's why she died."

The porch squeaks when he walks over to me. "Children and cats. I've never cared for either very much." I try to get back inside, but he stops me. Leaning against the screen door with a white hanky sticking out of his jacket pocket, he warns me. "Stay away from me and my affairs."

I won't, I tell him, eyeing my stake near the steps. Running. Grabbing it, I hold it high.

He is smiling when he shows his vampire teeth. When he laughs, it sounds like nighttime when the cats cry — evil, mean, and sad all at the same time. Taking the stake from me he asks if I want to be like him. When he holds on to my wrist, his fingers feel like hot ice. "It's not a good life, Octobia May. Being neither alive nor dead."

I reach for the Band-Aid on his face. The one covering up Juppie's scratches. Whispering in my ear, he tells me how he will turn me into a vampire, too. It will happen when I least expect it, he warns me. And I will never, ever see Auntie or my parents again. He takes off the ring. The one I thought he'd thrown in the river, and shows me the girl. "She was alive once, too."

He had the ring made for children like me, he says, who will not leave well enough alone. And are determined to annoy him to no end. He pulls me to him, twisting my arm until my knees hit the steps and I am kneeling down in front of him.

"Aunt Shuma! Somebody. Help!"

Bessie's door opens. *Click.*

Our door opens, too. "Do not fret, Octobia May."

I am trying to talk but the words won't come out.

"Oh, how I'll miss Juppie. She loved my matzo ball soup. Especially the tasty little dumplings." She fans a fly away. "Maybe if you came inside and told us one of your lovely stories, dear, I'm sure you would feel better."

"Didn't . . . Didn't you see him, Mrs. Loewenthal?" I mention Mr. Davenport's name. But he vanished as soon as the door opened.

"My, my, yes I did . . . earlier." She holds on to the pearl necklace around her neck. "It is certainly about time he had himself a little sun." She smiles. Closing the door, she talks about making him some gefilte fish. "Sweet, with mayonnaise."

Auntie and Mr. Buster don't sit with me long once they get back. It is almost lunchtime and Auntie needs to get into the kitchen. I am talking to her about Mr. Davenport, but she cannot take any more vampire talk today, she says, massaging her temples.

"But, Aunt Shuma —"

"Juppie was old, Octobia May. Eighteen. She lived all of her lives." She sees a rusted nail sticking from between the bricks and hammers it with the heel of her shoe.

"He's gonna kill me." I open my mouth wide. "Bite me like that woman last night." I think about my garlic and crosses. But nothing can save me now.

Kissing me on my cheek, she says, "You brave, Octobia May, sleeping with that cat all night. I see now that Juppie musta appreciated it." She squeezes my chin. "I spoke to Mr. Davenport this morning to check on that cat scratch."

I push past Mr. Buster and hug her. "You saw it, didn't you?"

Auntie wipes my sweaty forehead. "A nick from the dull razor he used yesterday. That's what did it." When I ask her if she made him take off the Band-Aid so she could see the scratch, she says she didn't. Then she does bring up the Negro children down south. Have I thought about them "one iota"? Mailed my letter or sent what I had promised? She shakes her head and talks of calling my parents. "So they can see how you squandering your freedom."

When Mr. Davenport is not troubling me, I will have time enough to think about those children. But not now, I think to myself. I've more important things to do. Auntie does, too. After all, she hasn't been reading me the newspaper at night. She's been sitting in the parlor with Mr. Buster — sipping tea.

Mr. Buster pats my hand. He wishes he could believe me, because he likes me so much. But nothing I am saying adds up, he tells me. "He's odd. That's true. But even Officer O'Malley . . ."

Officer O'Malley searched his room last night after Juppie died and did not find a thing. "Except a bit of an odd fellow who enjoys writing and his solitude."

My legs are wobbling when I walk in the house. My blouse is soaking wet from the heat of the day. Picking at the garlic under my bed, I put a whole clove under my tongue. Then I take a bath, even though it isn't Saturday. Afterward, I put on my prettiest Sunday dress. And the shoes Auntie says I can wear when the time is special enough. Sitting at my desk, I write a note on Mr. Davenport's paper — sticking it up my sleeve. Laying down with my eyes shut, I think about the note. Auntie will find it once I am on the other side — a vampire or a devil like him. For he will kill me tonight, I know it. Then she will know I was telling the truth.

20

BASEBALLS AND TRUE FRIENDS

"Jeepers creepers, Octobia May. I can't breathe." Jonah takes a feather pillow off my bed. Pressing it over his mouth and nose, he says he won't be staying long. "Your auntie says I'm the one to bring you to your senses." His chest puffs out. "You can't even smell my head with all the garlic in here."

They splashed Aqua Velva over Jonah's head after his haircut. But with garlic cloves hanging from my ceiling, stuffed in drawers, and lined up at my windowsill like knickknacks at the pawnshop — I cannot smell it.

He pinches his nose while he's speaking to me. He sits at the window seat. "Ain't it enough that you bald-headed?"

"I am not bald-headed. I have hair now — a coating anyhow."

He pulls open the window to take in a deep breath. "They'll whip my hide good, Octobia May — all those kids I'll have to take on from teasing you about the way you smell."

Auntie has had enough, she's been saying. Serving me food in my room. Smelling garlic from the hallway down to the basement is more than she can abide. I get in bed and slide underneath the covers. I spend a lot of time here nowadays. "I'm afraid, Jonah."

He turns his nose loose. "Ain't a scared bone in your scrawny little body, Octobia May. Everybody know that."

"Mr. Davenport." I lower my voice. "I think he's the devil."

Jonah cannot stop laughing.

"It's not funny!" I am up before I know it, hitting him here and there. "He killed Juppie. That lady. He'll kill all of us."

"Octobia May." Jonah stands up. "Didn't you say you died before?"

"I did die."

"Ain't graveyards and dead people your friends?"

"Yes."

"I do not believe you died for real, Octobia May. But I believe in you." He walks to the middle of my room and jumps, pulling on the last of Mrs. Loewenthal's pink yarn. I cut it. Pinned strips of it to garlic cloves and tacked them to my ceiling. Mrs. Loewenthal does not believe in vampires, but she gave me the yarn. Mrs. Ruby said I wasn't to tell Auntie she had any part in this. But she went to the store and bought me extra garlic. Enough to fill the bathroom sink.

Sitting in the middle of the floor. With pulled-down yarn and garlic all around me. I ask Jonah if he'd seen Mr. Davenport lately.

"Nope. He in his room, like always. I suppose."

"Feel." I hold Jonah's hand up to my heart. "It beats and beats, and worries me so."

"Octobia May. Who gonna prove he a killer, or vampire, or both, if you turn into a Chicken Little?"

"But, Jonah . . ."

He opens the window wide and sticks his head out. Talking into the air, he says, "I'll be right down to play with you and Charles Madison just this minute."

I walk over to the window. The boys swing their sticks at balls they throw in the air. "Y'all hear me?" Jonah asks.

"You can play with us tomorrow," Charles says, snickering. "Today you can fetch the balls from the bushes."

"Or hold back the traffic when they roll into the street," Henry says.

Jonah takes the case off my pillow and starts filling it with garlic cloves. "Don't worry about 'em, Octobia May. My good luck is over, that's all." He gives a little smile. "I don't mind fetching balls."

I ask about his Satchel Paige balls. Will he be letting those boys use them? Jonah had six balls. All Satchel Paige baseballs signed by Jonah with names of the Negro league teams he played for. He doesn't want to talk about his baseballs. He looks away from me. "Anyhow, they didn't mean all that much to me no way."

When he's done, he walks over to my dresser and picks up a picture of Juppie. "Maybe you ain't scared, Octobia May. Could be you're only sad." He sits beside me on the window seat. "Maybe you're thinking you ain't got no friends." He lays Juppie's picture on my lap. "But I'm your friend, Octobia May." His hands go around my shoulder. "Hair or not. Smelly or sweet. I like you, Octobia May. So does Bessie." He digs in his pocket and pulls out a picture. "She sent this." It's me and him by the graveside. In another picture, Bessie caught me squatting. *Click.* Buckling Juppie's best collar to the ribbons on her box.

I never did cry much when Juppie passed away. Not one tear did I lose when Auntie asked if she should throw her things away. "Since my second operation," I whisper, "Juppie's been in my bed day and night."

Jonah asks why I think Bessie never talks. "What good does it do," I say. "People don't listen to you anyway." Then I sniff my bed. I can still smell Juppie on my pillows and sheets. Even after Auntie washed them.

Jonah says his mother doesn't believe in having pets. But if he ever gets one, he will name her Juppie. He tugs at the corner of his shirt, offering it to me to wipe my tears.

Walking across the room, I hold on to Juppie's picture. Looking at her, I see the truth. I am sad that she died. Scared as I was the first time they dug into my heart.

Jonah closes the window. "Octobia May, I need a big win. I get scratched up plenty good, digging balls out weeds." Sitting beside me, he says he's been wondering about Mr. Davenport. He's the most peculiar vampire he ever heard of, he says. "Writing, sunning himself, living with a houseful of folks. It don't all make sense, do it, Octobia May?"

I follow him to the door.

He steps into the hall. "We can win big, if we find out the truth. Then I'll be the luckiest boy ever. Everybody will play with me." He holds his hand out to me. "Come, Octobia May. Come out that room. Let's me and you figure out what he's really up to."

I want to walk out with him. To run down to the basement. Or sit outside with Bessie. But I can't. "He'll get me."

Jonah's crooked eye fixes itself on me. "Then who will help me get my baseballs back from the river?"

"Oh, Jonah."

All of his Satchel Paige baseballs drowned by his new friends, he admits. "So we both need help, Octobia May. Not just you."

Before he closes my door he shares a secret with me. Something he found out by accident, when Bessie's mother came to get her hair done at Jonah's mother's house. "Bessie's got a dead brother. Killed in the Korean War. Guess you right. Dead is truly all around you, Octobia May."

I push the dresser in front of the door. Then sit boxes and a heavy chair on top of it, while I bite a piece of garlic, right through the skin. Tugging at the bedpost, I try to drag it over, too. It weighs a mountain, but I keep pushing. I have to.

21

NOR FOR ALWAYS

They carry Aunt Shuma's casket out the house. "Good riddance," she says, slapping dust off her hands. She polished the casket before they came for it, 'cause Mr. Lillie said he'd give her a few extra bucks if she did. Looking brand-new. Ready to be filled. The men slide it into a hearse. Aunt Shuma shuts the front door. "Now, remember, Octobia May. When the ladies come, be on your best behavior." She stoops down while she talks to me. "Do not mention vampires or the dead woman in white they found in the river. It was a coincidence." Auntie admires herself in the mirror. "Her neck was not bit up, now, was it?"

Auntie isn't the first to tell me about the body. I overheard Mrs. Ruby on the porch say they found a colored gal floating faceup in the river. I knew she had on white. I know she is the lady I saw on Clinton Avenue. Maybe the newspapers did not want to scare folks by mentioning the bite marks on her neck. I do not mention the woman to Auntie. Vampire and devil talk are behind me now. Besides, the Do Some Good Ladies Club is coming over any minute now. I need to get dressed.

I walk down our freshly scrubbed front porch steps. Opening the storm cellar doors, I go down to the basement. I stop at the spot where I found Juppie. And not once do I talk to my pretend servant friends. Or think about the Before Girls. That's all behind me now.

Kicking coals Auntie uses to heat the furnace, I move on. Then up the rickety staircase I go, until I'm in my room.

I take the long way now. Using the steps no one thinks about anymore. They go straight from the basement to the third floor. Aunt Shuma says I am feeling better because I am giving my imagination a rest and everyone else, too.

I come downstairs and find Auntie fussing with the silverware and plates. I turn in circles and my skirt spins, showing off my new slip. "You do not know one thing about being a girl." She stops my circles then stares at my feet. "I'm just letting you wear these shoes to make you feel better." My red patent leather shoes have a thick, stout heel. I click them like Dorothy in *The Wizard of Oz*, but I am still here and Juppie is still dead. Auntie folds down my socks. "Ready?" I pull on my lace gloves, wiggling my fingers, and sniff. I smell like Evening in Paris perfume, not garlic. I am being a different girl these days. Maybe because way deep down inside I am still scared. And sad.

The bell rings. It's Bessie and her camera, both dressed up. "Nice ribbon." It's crisp and pink, tied in a bow on her camera strap. Matching the bow in her hair, it goes nicely with the black-and-white polka-dot dress she has on.

No sooner than Bessie steps inside, the Do Some Good women begin to show up. I curtsy. Bessie stares. They walk past us into the house, trying not to notice my head.

The club meets once a week at someone's house. Aunt Shuma is their newest member, put on probation until she finds herself a husband. The ladies touch my head, filling me with questions and sometimes raising a hand to God, asking him to heal me every place that I'm lacking. They smile at Bessie. Jonah's mother whispers, "You know her brother's dead. Yes, sir. Shot in Korea. Uncle Sam should be ashamed."

Auntie looks shocked.

Jonah's mother folds her gloves over her purse. "Yes, indeedy. And she hasn't spoken a lick since."

Bessie crosses her feet at the ankles and hangs her head.

I take her by the hand. "Sometimes it's good not to talk, don't you think, Mrs. Nicholson?"

Using handkerchiefs to hide their mouths, a few of the ladies whisper to one another. Jonah's mother's lips tighten, before she says our block is getting quite an interesting reputation because of Bessie and me.

"Indeed." The doctor's wife clutches her purse.

Bessie's hand holds tight to her Brownie. Jonah's mother asks if she knows how to use it. And before we know anything, she is rushing everyone into the sitting room. Insisting that Bessie take their picture.

They pull out their compacts. And stare in the mirrors while they freshen their makeup. Auntie powders her nose. Jonah's mother puts red rouge on her cheeks. The other ladies do the same, while pinning their curls or tending to the garter belts that hold their stockings up.

"Sorry about your brother." I hold on to her hand again. "I never had one. But if I did . . ." I am quiet, but still thinking. If my brother died, I would be sad forever and ever. Then how could I talk? With all that sadness drying me up inside?

Finally all twelve of the ladies are ready. Sitting on the couch and armrest, they look serious and important.

Bessie's camera clicks and flashes. She moves in closer. Then backs up. *Pop* goes the flash again and again. Auntie wants me to be in the picture with the ladies.

Click.

Then I ask Bessie to sit with them.

"Cheese," I say, trying to cheer her up.

She smiles.

Click.

I'm telling the story this time.

22

NO MORE VAMPIRES

Jonah stands under the window stammering, with Bessie at his side. "Octobia May. Please." His mother is across the room, crocheting along with all the other ladies. He quiets his voice after I warn him. But he is begging me this time. I freeze when he brings up Mr. Davenport's name. Looking over my shoulder and out the window, I ask him to please hush. "This instant."

The ladies gossip and drink Maxwell House coffee, even though it is making them each sweat. "What's a Supreme Court again?" I ask when one of the ladies mentions it. Auntie has told me, but I forget.

Auntie explains. The doctor's wife says, "And praise be. For they will be the ones to help to truly set us free this second time."

"I'm free." I am glad to get away from Jonah and vampires. Walking over to the ladies I pick up a needle. "Auntie says I have as much freedom as I want."

"Well, it seems the rest of us Negroes ain't as free as you, Octobia May." Jonah's mother sips from her flowered cup. "Mr. Thurgood Marshall thinks so, too. He'll meet with the Supreme Court again in October. To make the judges see — once and for all — that separate ain't equal in schools down south, Kansas, and other places, too.

They mention some of the places up north, where we don't treat fairly — banks that won't lend to us or lend at sky-high rates, neighborhoods where we can't move, jobs off-limits to us, pools we can't swim in. But they will take the North any day, they all agree.

Auntie looks at me with disappointment in her eyes. "I know all about this," she explains. She's read about it to me more than once.

Jonah's mother holds up her cup for me to pour more coffee into. Snorting, she says, "If Mr. Marshall was a vampire. Well, then, I'd suppose you'd know all there was to know about him; those judges, too."

Jonah is still in the victory garden, standing between rows of cabbages, when Bessie and I go outside. I told

Auntie I needed fresh air, so she let me leave for a bit. And was glad for it. "I seen him, Octobia May." Jonah squashes ants carrying a potato peel across a pile of dirt. "Outside in all this here sun."

The heel of my foot taps the ground like I am keeping time to one of Jimmy Dorsey's famous songs.

"There's a long line of men downtown, and he's one of 'em. Not far from the river, Octobia May."

My throat squeezes, while my head wrestles with what he said. Day by day it seems Mr. Davenport is spending more time in the sun.

"Come. He won't hurt you, Octobia May. I won't let him." When I look up at Jonah, his crooked eye seems almost straight. "Please."

Minutes later, Jonah is running wide-legged up the street, far ahead of us. Just before Bessie and I round the corner, I slow to a stop. Afraid. My hand reaches out for hers. "Oh, Bessie."

She stares.

"Do not be sad about your brother," I whisper. "Juppie most likely has met him and is telling him what good friends we are now."

Jonah walks back and takes me by my other hand, squeezing.

"Let's go," I say, not turning their hands loose until we are walking close enough to the river to sit and wade in it.

113

Bend River was clear blue a long time ago. I pretend it's still that way today. That I can see to the bottom, where logs and frogs and thick cool mud sits for anyone who wants to see. It keeps me from being nervous and thinking about him.

Maybe Bessie is nervous, too. Her hand is sweating all over mine. Jonah is the brave one today. Running backward. Skipping ahead. He looks happy, like hundreds of shiny new nickels will be waiting for him when the day is done. "There." He points. "It's Mr. Davenport. Now, ain't it?"

Mr. Davenport is in line, that's for sure. The sign over his head says, YOUR COUNTRY NEEDS YOU. Rolling up his sleeves, he sits before laying down. The men in the beds beside him hold their arms out, too. When a Red Cross nurse sticks a needle in Mr. Davenport's arm, thick red blood goes up the tube, filling up the bag.

"He's got blood, Octobia May. Red American blood like the rest of us."

I swallow. "And vampires don't have blood. Do they, Jonah?"

"They do not."

Bessie takes my hand. I keep my eyes on the blood. His blood.

Before we leave, Jonah asks one of the Red Cross volunteers if he can give blood. Only men are giving blood today. "GIs who fought in World War Two." She

114

pinches his cheek. They are giving blood for American soldiers everywhere. We can help out in our own way, she says, by writing letters to soldiers, knitting them socks, or sending them candy. "I hear they love peanut brittle." She winks.

I tell her about Bessie's brother. "Any day now the last of our boys will be home from Korea," she says. "You can be proud, young lady. Your brother helped to keep us all safe."

Bessie smiles. Jonah salutes. I keep my eyes on him. Mr. Davenport, who is rolling down his sleeve, is looking at me.

23

AUNTIE ON HER OWN

Bessie's father is at the end our block, with his arms folded. He'd give me a piece of his mind, he says, but he is a gentleman and will not speak unkindly to a girl. Her mother's eyes apologize to me, when I say we went down to the river and I held Bessie's hand almost the entire time. When he and Bessie are just ahead of her, she whispers, "Thank you, Octobia May. I am seeing glimmers of my old Bessie, because of you."

I know about her son, I say, taking her hand. "I just bet he was wholesome, too."

She holds on to her belly, which is growing bigger day by day. "Wholesome and smart." But he snuck off and signed up for the war against their wishes. Bessie got the news first. "She was all alone when the War Department soldiers came." Her mother says the soldiers meant no harm. Walking away, they were whispering and she overheard them.

Her mother speeds up, heading for the porch. Bessie waves.

Inside the house, the women admire their work. They have piles of doilies. Pot holder doilies. Doilies that cover lamps, toilet rolls, ones that sit under drinking glasses or make your toilet bowl top look dignified and respectable. Lots of them were made before they all came. Today they get put in a box and sent to the old folks' home.

I sit at the organ with my legs crossed. Looking respectable, too. The doctor's wife likes to pick a secret out of you, little by little, like corn from between your teeth. She says she'd like to know where I've been this past hour.

How can I say I found Mr. Davenport being a good citizen right in the middle of town? It would only make them think I was telling tales all along. So I mention the Supreme Court. Just to distract them. And so they talk and talk.

There's a little Negro girl in Kansas who lives just a few blocks from a white school but they won't let her attend, I learn. She must go to the Negro school, which isn't nearly as nice. And walk through a railroad yard to catch a bus to get there. So her family is suing and the Supreme Court is wondering what it can do to help her. This makes all the grown-ups very happy. "Freedom everywhere. For everyone," a few ladies shout. Only they do not want too much freedom for me.

What does a little girl do all alone on the streets late at night anyway, they want to know. They call me a gadabout and laugh when they talk about vampires chasing after me. "It isn't funny!" I shove my hand so close to Jonah's mother's face that I bump her in the nose.

"Ill-mannered. Rude. That's what you are. No wonder the devil's hightailing it after you."

Auntie gently changes the subject. She is thinking of hiring extra help. A sixteen-year-old girl from Georgia, who wants to finish her education up north.

Mrs. Stefford is the wife of the chauffeur who drives for the president of S and L Bank. "Why can't you find yourself a husband to help you manage your affairs?" She thinks Auntie should sell our place. Times are changing. Negroes can earn money in more responsible ways, she believes.

Auntie pats her lap and lets me sit on it. She rocks me for a minute, to calm herself more than me, I believe. "Y'all talking change. Well, this here child won't need no husband to pay her way in the world. That look like change to me." She pats my hand. "She'll go to college.

And finish." Auntie didn't. "I'll have a string of hotels all over this land with her name on each one. Even in the South. Just wait and see."

Auntie tells them that she has been to almost every bank in this city. The answer to her dreams is always the same. They don't lend to unmarried women. And they only lend Negro couples money to buy houses in certain parts of town.

She looks at the chauffeur's wife. "Can your husband help me? Maybe put in a good word with the president of that bank? I ain't talked to those folks yet." Auntie tells them her plan. She will buy three more boarding houses. Keep them going for a few years. Save the profits. Build her own hotel. Then a few more. They cringe when she says she will even own a hotel in Alaska.

Mrs. Stefford thinks this is no time to bother Mr. Harrison, because his colored help keeps turning up dead. "First the cook. Now the maid has been found floating upstream."

Have they heard the scuttlebutt? the doctor's wife wants to know. About the teller who went missing three years ago. "White. Young fella." He was not from here. Not from money, so the newspapers didn't make much of it. But people are recalling it now, she says.

Pouring the chauffeur's wife the last of the coffee, Auntie asks if she might come past her house sometime, to discuss things with her husband. She picks at the wart on her knuckle. "Sometimes I believe them bankers listen better when you got a man sitting next to you."

Jonah's mother stands and asks Auntie why she thinks anyone would lend her their husband. Then she mentions that she knows the bank president herself. She works some of his parties in her spare time. Cooking, serving, and cleaning. She asks if Auntie thinks she should introduce her to the president, too.

The other ladies daintily sit their napkins on tables; their china cups and saucers on Auntie's silver tray. Aunt Shuma is still talking when they all begin to gather their things and leave. Including Jonah's mother, who gives her regrets for the way Auntie "tries to impose herself on folks."

Auntie sees them to the door. Our boarders stay where they are, upstairs in their rooms. Being quiet.

Carrying a handful of forks into the kitchen, Auntie says, "Snobs." She throws them in the sink. "Scared as hens with a fox on their trail." She wraps her warm arms around me. "Octobia May. You got more bravery in your kneecap than all them grown women got put together."

I hug her tight.

"They primp and sit, waiting for someone else to make their lives more comfortable." Reaching up to the window, she grabs her hammer. "I make my own life better." They misunderstood her, she tells me. She didn't want Mrs. Stefford's husband to talk for her. Just to walk into the bank and make the introductions. Sit down and be quiet while she tended to her own business. I ask why she doesn't ask Mr. Buster. He would go. "Bankers would not take kindly to a man wearing yellow shoes."

I stay put while she ties an apron around my waist. "Don't you wanna be married, Auntie? I do."

She talks about being married once, at eighteen. Her poppa had it annulled. She busies herself with the dishes. "So I am getting all that I can get on my own. Ain't mad at the married ones — just ain't married."

I dry the teacups that she hands me. She talks to me about the hotels she will build. She is thinking of building the first one down south. "Land's cheaper. And colored folks got it harder there."

I salute her. "You are brave, Auntie. As brave as a soldier."

She salutes me, too. "We brave," she says, winking. "Not afraid of vampires or taking a chance in life. Are we?"

"No. We not afraid of nothing." I relax and look at the ceiling. Not even Mr. Davenport and all his secrets, I think.

Auntie is staring down at me and smiling like my head is full of long, brown, wavy curls hanging down to my knees. "And if we do get scared, it ain't gonna be for long, nor for always — will it, Octobia May?"

"No. Nor for always," I say, feeling my heart sing.

24

A LUCKY BREAK

"Who's that?" Sitting up, I reach for one of the screwdrivers in my bed. "Don't come in my room."

"Octobia May, it's Sunday. Ain't you ready? You the one that wanted to go to the funeral parlor and look over them bodies." Jonah turns and twists the knob. "Did you forget?"

I look outside at the sunny day, then at six screwdrivers — small and tall — sitting beside my pillow. Rushing over to the door in my gown, I unlock it. "Morning, Jonah." Then I'm off to my bed again; back under the blanket.

Pulling at the wool blanket, he says, "Are you the

old Octobia May who ain't scared of nothing, or the new one who's getting on my last nerve with her skittishness?" He sits on the side of my bed. "He's no vampire, Octobia May."

"I know."

Whispering, he tells me, "Guess whose door is swung wide open?" He pulls at his tie. "Wide enough for the whole world to come inside and have a look around."

I am up in a flash. Dressed without washing or brushing my teeth. Wearing the same undershirt I slept in, I apologize to Auntie and Momma in my head. I was raised better, but I do not have time to freshen up. Getting back into his room is the most important thing. "Come along, Jonah."

We are good tiptoers. Making it to the second-floor landing without a sound. Auntie's yelling stops us in our tracks. "Octobia May. Mr. Buster ain't waiting all day. If you plan to work with him, get moving, girl."

I was feeling rather poorly all morning. I had the blues over Juppie. I went to see the Before Girls yesterday and could not muster the strength to see my own cat. I knew I shouldn't be in the graveyard, but I snuck in anyhow. But the news about Mr. Davenport's room was just what I needed. I have been thinking about him lately. Giving blood like any decent person with a heart. But why?

We make our way inside Mr. Davenport's room, with Jonah calling his name. "Mr. Daven . . . port. Can we —"

He forgets what I told him to say just a second ago, so I finish for him. "Mr. Davenport, Auntie asked me to bring you these towels. We know you usually take care of your own laundry but —" Walking in circles we both look up and down and around. "Good. He really is out someplace, Jonah." I step into his living room. He's the only one that has one, plus his very own private bath.

I hold up his underwear. He irons them. Auntie never would. A single woman can't handle a man's personal things. Jonah picks up Mr. Davenport's shaving brush and mug. Holding the straight razor, he pretends to shave his own face.

"If you're dead you can't grow hair on your face or under your arms, can you, Jonah?" I should have known all along, I say.

I'm not to concern myself too much, he tells me. I was tricked into thinking what I thought. He moves to the other side of the room. "To throw you off his trail."

Jonah sits at Mr. Davenport's desk with his fingers on the typewriter keys.

"No — Auntie would hear."

Opening and closing his desk drawers, I examine what's inside. An old dirty map of Belgium. Nothing important. Jonah pulls open the next drawer. A ribbon that looks like it's missing a medal. Maybe from a race he'd won. A scrap of paper sits in the corner of the last drawer. Words. Capitalized and crossed out. Make us scratch our heads. *The Rhineland Campaign. The Ardennes. Bastogne. Wereth. The Third Reich. Belgium.*

Jonah sits at the desk with his feet up. Leaning back. Resting his head on his arms, he says he's figured out what Mr. Davenport's been hiding. "That he's a communist."

"A communist?"

His mother has been listening to a man on the radio. "McCarthy." He says that communists are everywhere in America and we have to get rid of them. I know they could fly over and drop radiation on us one day. But I did not know they lived here.

"He's a spy, Octobia May. For . . . for . . . for the communists, that's right." Jonah opens more drawers. Then heads for the closet.

I am right behind him until I notice a trash can full of ashes. I knew I smelled something burning the other day, but Auntie would not let me investigate. "Jonah." I pick up the only piece of paper that survived. *Boys of War*, it says, *written by Hardy Dav . . .* The rest of his name is burned away.

Jonah says it must not have been very good if he took a match to it.

"I'd never burn my stories," I say. "People will want to read them one day."

Skipping into the closet, I ignore Auntie's calls to get downstairs.

25

MR. DAVENPORT'S SECRET
TREASURES

Using a step stool, Jonah reaches for Mr. Davenport's hats and tries one on. He sure is a fancy dresser for a communist, Jonah thinks.

On the top shelf, I find a picture with a tie clip on it. Faded. Four kids are standing in front of an old wooden lean-to. Two Negro children — a girl and a boy — are sitting on the steps without shoes. A white boy, with his arm around his colored friend, leans in close. He's telling him a secret, so we can only see part of his face. One eyeball — and a scar over his left brow.

"It's his." I open my hand and hold the tie clip out to him. "See. It's in the picture." The boy with the blond curls is wearing a tie.

"Hey!"

I cover Jonah's mouth with my hand. "Quiet."

"And that's Mr. Davenport. When he was our age."

I hand Jonah the clip and the picture. But who is this? we both wonder.

"Mr. Davenport's got millions of secrets," I tell Jonah. "So many he wouldn't mind killing me to keep 'em. Or you. Maybe he killed him, too." I look over the boy's face. He's smiling, but it's a trick smile. Happy-looking, but sad around the edges.

We keep looking, hoping to find more things to help us get to the truth about Mr. Davenport. Jonah's fingers and mine dig through pocket after pocket. But it's a metal box at the back of the closet, sitting under boxes and boxes of shoes, that gives us our biggest clue.

"Why would he need a box filled with sand anyhow?" Jonah asks, digging inside it.

I am trying to be careful, but I spill sand, too. Plenty. Especially after I lift the money out.

I hand Jonah a bill, wondering where the box was before. He picks up another hundred and fans himself with two fifties.

"Eight, nine — hundred." I stop counting. They are new bills. As crisp as the shorts Mr. Davenport irons.

Auntie is counting, too. Saying this will be the last time she summons me. And that I should know by now I will not be going with Mr. Buster.

Digging deeper I find more treasures. A diamond necklace. A bracelet filled with green stones. But not the girl on the ring. "Do communists . . . steal money and —"

"Murder people?" He says what is on my mind. And swallows. "Maybe, Octobia May. Mr. McCarthy says they do all sorts of things. But mainly they are not good and true Americans."

I think about Mr. Davenport. He is not being a true-blue American. Maybe he is a communist. Or just a spy. Is a communist the same as a spy? I ask Jonah. He isn't sure.

"Get down here, girl!"

Using one of Mr. Davenport's handkerchiefs, we take the necklace, two fifty-dollar bills, and scraps of paper — proof. Closing the box. We put things back in place and try to brush away the sand. That doesn't work so well, so we blow it.

Running from the closet to Mr. Davenport's bathroom, I point to an old laundry chute. Jonah scoots in headfirst. I shove him. And down he goes. It's a small, tight space, meant for blankets and sheets, not girls and boys. My head bounces like a ball along the way. Jonah yells like he's riding high on the Ferris wheel.

I stash the things in the furnace just before Auntie comes downstairs. Pulling each of us by our ears, she forbids Jonah from returning to her house ever again. Then she locks me in my room.

At suppertime, I am served a tray of lukewarm tea, fried potatoes, and cold chicken. "But, Auntie —"

"I am finished. With all the talking and guiding."

"But what did I do?"

She stands at my door ten minutes naming all that I've gotten myself into. This very day Mr. Davenport is out arranging for her to meet with the president of S and L Bank, she says, "and you break into his room." She was airing it out, I learn. Giving blood again yesterday had made him sick and he'd made a mess of his room, asking her to tend to it.

Auntie says she needs to send me back home to learn what every girl should know. How to knit, iron, and sew. Make a proper meal, set a good table. Care for children. Look out for the indigent and the poor. And be a good wife. Her back is to me when she says these things. Perhaps that way I will settle down some, and learn to obey when I'm told, I hear.

I walk over to the window and peek out. "But you said . . ." Tears run down my cheeks. "I was free to do like I wanted."

She darts across the room as fast as an arrow. "What you know about freedom, child? After all the free I've given you. Tell me that."

I am thinking too long, I suppose, because she leaves without my answer.

I do not eat the food she brought to me. Or think about Mr. Davenport or worry over Jonah and never seeing him again. With my pencil and my notebook, I write one big word at the top of my page. *Freedom*. I think I won't see it for a very long time.

26

BOARDER STORIES

"Three whole weeks and no Octobia May. I feel like I, too, am being punished." Mrs. Loewenthal opens her arms wide. "Now, how many hugs do you have for me this fine morning? Three weeks' worth, at least, I hope."

I am in her warm arms, slobbering up her black sweater with my tears. Happy that Mrs. Ruby is not too far behind, I run to her and do not mind her kisses wetting up my forehead.

They both sit on my bed. Side by side. Mrs. Loewenthal taking my hand. Do I know what I've done, she asks. "Taken the joy out of supper." Without my stories she says they are forced to gossip about neighbors and family, and that is never a good thing.

"Or worry over our aches and pains." Mrs. Ruby's wrinkled fingers find her swollen knee. "If only you'd behave, Octobia May."

Before I know it Miss Marble has made her way into my room. "Behave. With that devil of a man downstairs inspiring her to discover his secrets?"

Mrs. Loewenthal's pockets are always full of butterscotch candy. She pulls out a handful. I choose first. Then she shares with the rest.

"What's it like?" I unwrap the candy.

They all look at me curiously.

"Outside, I mean. I don't even know what color the sun is anymore."

They get a good hardy laugh out of that. I even see their bellies jiggle. They have spoken to Auntie repeatedly, they say, and she is firm in her thoughts that I had to be punished extra hard so I knew what I have been doing wasn't right.

I want to tell them about the money and other treasures, but I'm afraid they will turn against me, too. "She says I do not know anything about freedom." I walk across the room and lay on the floor.

Mrs. Loewenthal nods. "Negroes and Jews. So long we seek freedom. So hard a thing for us to find, it appears. People have always tried to keep it from us."

"Like how Auntie doesn't want me to be free."

The whole room is silent. The ladies' faces look different but the same. Mrs. Loewenthal says, "Tsk, tsk, Octobia May. Maybe Shuma is right."

Mrs. Ruby asks if I am the same girl she's known all this time. Because if I were I'd know I am "the most privileged Negro child in the neighborhood."

I do not like to disappoint them, but I have. Curling up in my grandpap's chair across from them, I apologize. They each pull out a story. And beg me not to pull out any of my own. Mrs. Ruby talks about her mother. She saw the Union soldiers march into town on horseback when she was eight. She sits up tall and proud, holding on to the charm necklace her granny left her. "Now, why were they there, Octobia May?"

"The soldiers?" I know I should know. My parents had talks with me about some things. But I don't much care about wars. Or stories that aren't in books.

"To free the slaves, like my mother. So Negroes today could live and work wherever they want. Do whatever we think we were born to do."

For the first time in a long time, I think of the Negro kids down south without Auntie's encouraging me. What about them? I ask. "They're not able to do all that they want."

Miss Marble agrees. "All Negroes ain't free, north or

south. Lots more needs to be done to equal things out in this world."

Mrs. Loewenthal mentions first coming to America. "So big. So many different kinds of food, people, neighborhoods. A wonderful place to live. To be free, but not always so wonderful I soon learned." She takes Mrs. Ruby's hands. "Too many signs, businesses, groups speaking hate."

"No Catholics, Negroes, or Jews . . ." Mrs. Ruby shakes her head.

Mrs. Loewenthal and Miss Marble finish her sentence. "Only Gentiles need apply."

"Oh, I seen it time and time again." Miss Marble crosses her arms when she talks about the time she, a rabbi, and his wife had to use the freight elevator to get inside a hotel.

I frown.

"A dirty, filthy elevator they used to haul broken furniture, trash, foul-smelling garbage, and God knows what. They made us take that! Plenty other hotels did, too. 'Cause people like us wasn't fit to walk in through the front door, they figured."

I listen while they talk about other troubles that have landed on the doorstep of Negroes and Jews in our country. Then Miss Marble brings up the Germans.

When Mrs. Loewenthal begins to rock, I know it's the war that is drawing her near. "They took our freedom from us a little at a time. Until we were fleeing. Or trapped in the ghettos, starving. And still others . . ." She whispers her aunts' names. Then opens her eyes.

I am glad, I say, that they did not hurt her. But she says what happens to one Jew, happens to all Jews. "If we remember that, we will stay free."

I repeat what she says, but it comes out different. "What happens to one person . . ."

We all finish the second line together. "Happens to all people."

Mrs. Loewenthal is the first to stand to leave. "I like that, Octobia May."

They all do.

One by one, they kiss my forehead and sit dimes on my dresser. "A girl has always got to have a little something saved up for herself," Mrs. Ruby says. She tucks her arm through Mrs. Loewenthal's. With aching legs, they all waddle out like ducks.

Sitting by the window, I watch Bessie playing alone across the street. Free.

27

HOW TO CATCH A MURDERER

Jonah and I divided up the money. Not for keeps. But so Auntie or Mr. Davenport would not find it in one place.

I sleep with my dresser in front of my door sometimes. Just in case he takes it upon himself to come for his treasures. The picture. The tie clip. The words on paper. They all hold a secret, I think. Last night, I wrote a story about the girl and the boy in the picture. They were holding hands so I think they are the best of friends.

It's been a month in all I've been on punishment, with only Bessie across the street for company. Not that she could come by and visit. But when I serve our boarders their meals or drinks on the porch, she is always sure to be outside taking pictures. Auntie did mind that part, but then felt poor Bessie needed to busy herself somehow. And staying on her side of the block and taking pictures did not seem like a big, tall thing. But today it will be different. I'm free. And Bessie, Jonah, and I will be together again.

Mr. Davenport was busy all the while I was being punished. I could hear him typing more than ever — maybe he's writing another book. His door crept open day by day. But I do not know where he went. My notebook is full of his comings and goings. Sometimes I'd wonder, do communists have meetings? I've been asking Auntie questions about them, too. She says I do not have to worry, there are no communists around here.

"Mr. McCarthy thinks they are like ants, hiding in plain sight."

She laughed. And was sure as she is Negro, she said, "That McCarthy man is making a fool of himself. And America, too."

Picking Auntie's tomatoes, I watch the ants working. And listen to Mr. Buster try to sweet-talk Auntie.

"Shuma." Mr. Buster shoves his hands deep in his pockets. "Ever go to the picture show?"

Before she can answer, Auntie is hurrying me into the house to freshen up. We are going shopping today. I wash my wet forehead and my sweaty legs. She pinches my cheek. "I am thankful for your turnabout. And the letter shows you learned a thing or two up there."

Auntie's right. I learned my lesson. Every night I read the Negro paper until my eyes hurt. After supper in my room, I would sit at my desk. With a pen and a piece of paper, I wrote letters. Only showing Auntie the one I liked best. It's to the girl they won't let in the school in Kansas. The paper had her name and address.

Dear Linda Carol Brown, I began.

I am sorry that you are not all the way free. I will write a letter to President Eisenhower. I have plenty of time to do it because I am on punishment. I will say "please free the Negroes in Kansas, Down South, Washington D.C., Delaware, and any Negroes Up North that need their freedom, too."

By the way. Do you have any Jews living down there? We have Mrs. Loewenthal living with us. Her people were free, but then the Nazis rounded some of them up and put them into concentration camps and gassed them.

I think people should be nice to all people. I think that Mr. Thurgood Marshall, and the Supreme Court will get you into that school. What happens to one person happens to all people. So if you get in, other

Negroes will get to go to the schools they want. Jews will get to live anywhere they like. The Irish and Italians, who Auntie says sometimes get called names, will all be better off, too. And I can grow up and be a detective — like I am thinking of being these days — without anybody telling me no.

Well, I hope you are having a good day. My punishment ends tomorrow, so I will be free. By the way, do you believe in vampires? I used to. But now I know Auntie is right. People at the movies made them up, so we would pay to go to the picture show.

Your friend,
Octobia May

P.S. School begins for me next week!

28

BESSIE AND THE BAD MEN

Once a month on Saturday, Auntie and I go shopping for anything she does not grow. Jonah and Bessie are going with us today. Mr. Buster asks to come along, but Auntie says no. Then she brings up the picture show, I guess because he looks sad. "It might be nice. I do work a lot."

Smiling, he mentions the new shoes he bought. He did not get the brown ones Auntie recommended. That color is too quiet for him, he says. "You like lavender, Shuma?"

Auntie's eyes practically jump out of her head. "At times . . . Easter colors suit a person just fine, I imagine."

We are headed for the bus stop when the iceman's truck pulls onto our street. "Fifteen or thirty?" he asks Auntie. She wants thirty pounds of ice since no more can be delivered until Monday. He walks into our house to put it in the icebox and grabs the money from the cookie jar once he's done. Then off shopping we go.

Jonah, Bessie, and me go from stand to stand, sampling cut watermelon, and pickles swimming in a wooden barrel.

Auntie walks ahead of us. "Fresh fruit . . . fresh! Freshhhh fish. Whitings. Porgies. Heads on or tossed," the man shouts. "Apples . . . sweet as your girlfriend . . . Melons . . . come taste and see . . . Cabbage, carrots, strings beans, butter beans, no better beans than bought from me."

Auntie haggles with him, trying to get the lowest price. She pays for a dozen crabs, six pieces of fish with the heads left on, and all the okra he has left. She'll pick it up before we leave, then go home and make okra stew, she says.

Our next stop is a shop filled with boxes and bundles of ties. Bow ties. Colored, silk, cotton, and new ties. Used ones, too. Ties across a curtain rod block the sun from shining through the store window. Knotted ties on mannequins without heads make Bessie smile.

Click.

The lady at the sewing machine is stitching together a pumpkin-orange-colored tie. Jonah takes out one of our fifty-dollar bills. "I want a tie." Before I can stop him he orders four more.

"No! We can't spend that money. It's not ours."

He says he is tired of me being the boss. While I was on punishment, he did some changing, too. "My friends and me —"

"What friends?"

"My friends and me are going to school the first day with brand-new ties. I decided before I came."

The lady sits each tie in tissue paper, then puts them into fancy boxes fit for kings. Each tie costs seventy-five cents. Jonah won't give the rest of the money back to me even when I ask him. "Satchel Paige would be so mad at you, Jonah," I say, rushing out of the store.

Sixth Street is busy as a hive. People are all around us, as crowded as popcorn in a bowl. Arguing. Buying. They pull shopping carts full of food. Sacks of sugar. Hunks of meat wrapped in brown paper. Live crabs scratching inside of bags.

Jonah won't quit following me. Bessie can't keep up. Looking at Mr. Davenport's picture. I think about the boy with the tie. Where was he going? Why wasn't Mr. Davenport dressed up, too? Did they go to school together? Sit by one another in class? I carry the picture and tie clip on me all the time now. He may find it if I hide it someplace else.

"Octobia May!" Jonah's voice stops me in my tracks.

"If it's stolen money, why can't we spend it?" He looks over his boxes and frowns. "Something good might as well come of it."

The right thing to do, I tell Jonah, is to return the ties and get the money back. He wants to know what I will do with my share of the loot. I don't know. I do not want Mr. Davenport to have it. I think he has bad plans for it anyway. Jonah will not return the ties. But he promises to hold on to the rest of the money until I say what I'll do with mine.

Click.

Bessie takes a picture of us arguing. I'd like to break that camera in two. Instead I ask if she wouldn't mind thinking of something helpful and useful to do with the money. "What about me?" Jonah looks like I hurt his feelings.

"We'll all three come up with something," I say. "And choose the best way to go."

When we get to the corner where the Gypsy reads palms for fifteen cents and a man is roasting peanuts in shells, Jonah stops. "Look, Octobia May."

Just ahead of us, a woman sitting in a cart is being pulled by a boy Jonah's age. "Not her," he says. "Him." Jonah turns my head in the other direction.

"Mr. Davenport."

Click.

He is walking up the street biting into a big, juicy red apple. Talking to a white man. They are both dressed in black suits. With white shirts and gold cuffs that shine. His hat isn't straw. It's black, too. Even from here I can tell it's all very expensive. "Maybe he bought those things with that stolen money, Jonah."

We follow them. Stepping over rotten prunes. Walking by pigeons with bread in their beaks, I stop. And we all hide between wooden stands full of vegetables and packages of food. When they turn the corner, we do, too.

"Octobia May —"

"Quiet, Jonah."

"But . . ." Jonah stands up. "I know that man."

Jonah does not know how to speak quietly. His voice jumps over all the others here and taps Mr. Davenport on the shoulders. Setting his eyes on us tight as magnets, he throws down his apple. Jonah waves, but then he sees what I see in Mr. Davenport's eyes. A warning.

Click.

Bessie is the brave one today. She steps into the cobblestone street. Walking past a man with a cart full of flowers, she stops.

Click.

144

Mr. Davenport tries to grab the camera. Bessie runs. Past Mr. Abe, the dollar-a-week man selling pots out the trunk of his car. Between two pavement stands where wool suits are on sale. Past the woman with the talking parrot.

"Hardy!" Mr. Davenport's friend calls his name.

Click.

Out of breath, Bessie sits at the curb in front of us.

Mr. Davenport and his friend turn up Leaning Alley. They look back and speed up.

"Now what you all up to?" Auntie wants to know, when she finds us. We don't get to answer before she is rushing off again. "Now for them chickens."

I do not say another word. I walk up the street beside her, with Bessie holding my hand and Jonah saying that man sure does look familiar. "He somebody important, too. If only I could remember where I seen him before."

29

AUNTIE AND THEM CHICKENS

The sign overhead says, JOE'S CHICKENS AND CHICKS. The tiny bell over the door dings when people walk in. Colored and white fill up the shop, picking out the best of the chickens. "Coming in?" Auntie wants to know. Jonah and Bessie stay outside and sit on the steps. I tell them to be on the lookout for Mr. Davenport, while I go inside to try and save them chickens.

Sometimes I see pastors in here wearing their white collars and looking the chickens over. I like that. Before you die, you should know for sure that God is looking out for you.

The chickens sit in cages with other cages sitting on

top and beside them. They all talk at the same time. I hear them in my mind. *Get me out of here. Don't kill me. I don't want my throat slit.* I reach through the cage, rubbing feathers. Picking up feed. Letting the chickens eat from my fingers, I say, "Mr. Lioni, do you *have* to dunk them in scalding-hot water?"

He is weighing a chicken. The wings flap, fighting to get free. "Octobia May, you no gonna bother to me this day. Are you?" He blows the feathers apart while he looks for sores and bugs. "You gonna alike this one," he says to a customer, kissing his fingers. "It'll make ya . . ."

"I wouldn't want my head cut off."

Auntie covers my lips with her hands. The woman at the scale says she does indeed want the head off, so she can make soup with it.

Auntie gives me a choice. Go outside and sit on the stoop with Jonah and Bessie and wait quietly. "Or stay and see that life ain't easy for chicken nor child." I watch chickens walk around in cages, looking worried. Some eat. Others move their eyes side to side, nervous. Mr. Lioni goes into the back room. The chicken screams from the hot water. I cover my ears.

Auntie uncovers them for me. "You know the routine."

When the head gets chopped off, the feet still kick. Three of Auntie's fingers go up once he's done wrapping the other order. "I'm sorry." I kneel down, patting another chicken. "I won't eat your cousins."

Auntie says she's had enough. "Chicken is your favorite and every time we come here you say the same thing." She points to the cages. "Fried up they don't seem so pitiful, I guess."

On their way to the back, I wave at the chickens. I tell their friends that I will not eat them, but that is not exactly true. Chicken tastes better than sweet cake. I eat it slow and even suck the marrow from the bones. It's just that I hate this part, coming here, knowing that they are so cute and soft. Auntie's chickens get wrapped and put in her grocery bag. Still warm.

She sighs. "I guess I can see how it might bother you. Seeing 'em alive one minute. Hearing how they end." Outside she picks strawberries off a cart, handing one to each of us. "But life is a hard road sometimes, Octobia May." She brings me because she says a businesswoman must make hard decisions in life. "She cannot pass up opportunities. Sometime they only come once." Auntie gives Jonah and Bessie two cents each to wander around for a while and get themselves something sweet. Comforting me, she says she will rethink me shopping for chickens. Not much bothers me so maybe she can respect my wishes on this, she thinks. Biting her bottom lip, she tells me she found Mr. Alexander's note the other day, behind the bushes. "I was disappointed in you."

I stop in my tracks.

She had a talk with him about Mr. Davenport working at the graveyard. "Octobia May, Mr. Davenport don't work there. You was right." Auntie takes me by the hand. "I do not believe in vampires. But I do believe in folks telling the truth."

"Auntie," I tell her for the first time, "I know he's not a vampire."

She hugs me, saying she is glad to know I've come to my good senses once and for all. I ask if she will toss Mr. Davenport out. Under her breath, so only I can hear, she talks about the bank. Tuesday two weeks hence, the two of them will go to the bank. During my school lunch break I am to meet her there. My generation's future will be different than any colored girl's ever, she tells me. "You must be prepared . . . for that kind of freedom." So she's making a hard choice, she says. To let him stay, in spite of things.

I have been trying to behave. To handle freedom like the grown-ups want me to. But if I see Mr. Davenport at the bank, maybe I won't do so good. Even now I want to chase after him — to shake his secrets free. "I don't want to go to the bank, Auntie. Mr. Davenport might get mad . . . if he sees me."

Holding her purse tight, she puffs up. "Mr. Davenport do not run my house. And how you gonna know how to take care of your own grown-up business, unless you see me taking care of mine?"

Jonah waves, telling me to come see what I want and

he will buy something we both can enjoy. Handing me a penny, Auntie waves me on. Jonah, me, and Bessie walk the back streets together. Until I see something so wonderful and special, I dart off, leaving the two of them behind. "Satchel Paige!"

They see the sign now, too. Satchel Paige baseball cards — '48 and '53. Jonah flies inside the drug store. "He plays for the St. Louis Browns, Octobia May. You can buy his cards way out there, or near about, but not so much here. It's my lucky day."

Bessie sits her penny on the counter. I do the same, then Jonah. Carefully, the man hands him the card. Jonah begins to read the back of the card and all the great things Mr. Paige has done. "Octobia May. Ain't he something else?"

"The best ever," I say, smiling at Jonah.

Auntie frowns at the card when we catch up to her. For five cents, you can buy a pack of baseball cards with three inside, plus a hunk of bubblegum inside to boot.

Walking ahead of us, Jonah keeps his eyes on Mr. Paige. He should have bought the 1948 card, I say. Jonah shakes his head. "One is enough — when it's the real, true thing that is."

Click.

I take Jonah and Bessie's picture. He's holding up the baseball card. She's wearing a tie. I am happy they are both my friends.

30

BESSIE'S FATHER AND THE FIRST DAY OF SCHOOL

On the way to school, one of the boys elbows Jonah in the side, asking him about his crooked eye. With Henry egging him on, the new guy says Jonah should put a patch over his eye like a pirate so people do not have to look at it. I give him a good hard shove. "Pick on somebody your own size." When the boy puts his fist up, I shove him again.

Jonah looks smaller than usual. Embarrassed. With his crooked eye doing its best to stare me down, he says, "Doggone you, Octobia May. I am free to take care of myself." He gives me worse than I gave the boy — a shove so hard I fall onto my bottom.

"Good job," the boys say, slapping Jonah on the back.

"We don't want girls around us anyhow," another one says, putting his arm over Jonah's shoulder.

A girl walking past stops to help me up. Brushing off my pants, she asks why I am not wearing a skirt or dress. It's the rule. I look around at all the coloreds and whites. And see that there's only one girl on her way to school in slacks — me.

Checked blouses. Taffeta dresses. Stripes. Plaids. Ruffles. It's all around me — starched and ironed, along with straw purses, pearls, and girls with fresh-pressed curls that shine like the sun.

Auntie was not smiling when I left home. Pants are what I wanted to wear. She let me, but like the time she cut my hair, she said I would regret it. Jonah looks me up and down dissatisfied, I see, with my cuffed dungarees, flannel shirt, and the plaid bow in my hair. It's grown a tad bit. I join Jonah and his friends. But they speed up. In line in the schoolyard, one of them says, "Hey. How much money did you say you got?"

I can see Jonah dig deep into his pocket. He and his friends watch my bow drop onto the ground. I leave it. It wasn't holding on to much anyhow. "Octobia May," Jonah says, "she ain't so bad. Just don't know her place, is all." Then he hands the boy Mr. Davenport's money; some of it anyhow.

"Ten dollars!" one boy shouts. The other boys gather around Jonah. He tells them to be quiet, that there's more where that came from. This time I shove him and take off running when he hits the ground. It's not my intention, but I end up at the graveyard. It's been a while since I've been here. Or talked to Juppie or my friends.

"Lordy." I sit down my composition book and pencil. "I can see you all missed me." I pull weeds from between my friends' graves. Carry fountain water back and forth to a flower I once planted. The Before Girls thank me. The mayor asks where I've been. I listen carefully to him tell me how much fun they are having with Juppie. Walking over to her grave, I cry.

"Auntie kept her promise, didn't she, Juppie?" Reading her tiny headstone for the first time, I see that Auntie put me down as Juppie's loving mother. She said she'd make the headstone when she had a spare minute. Most likely she did it when I was on punishment. I was free to let her go into the ground like any old raggedy alley cat, Auntie told me before then. "Or let folks know she had some big-hearted kin in this world." I told her to make the wooden headstone. Now I see how much she thought of Juppie, too.

When the school bell rings, I take off. Running up Glory Lane. Tripping over my feet when I cut through Sunrise Road, I stop to catch my breath. "Octobia

May!" It's Mr. Alexander. I pick up steam. "Didn't I tell you —"

"I didn't do much, Mr. Alexander."

I am almost in the building when the principal comes for me. Holding on to my ear, she talks to me all the way to her office. I am wearing a dress, once I leave her. One that she keeps in her office, "for such an occasion."

Crinoline is no girl's friend. Nor are thick-soled shoes one size too big. I'd rather wear my own. She said they were more fit for a farm. And let me know she planned to stop by Auntie's this evening and have a talk with her. Carrying a purse, I am not in a good mood when I sit down in Bessie's father's class — in between her and Jonah's seats.

Mr. Amadeo goes over the rules again, for my sake, he says, because he never wants to put someone in the cloakroom on punishment unless he has to. I have my hands folded tight. My eyes look straight ahead. At least I'll be able to tell Auntie a few things I did right today.

31

BESSIE'S FATHER'S CLASS

Bessie's father pulls down the rolled-up map. And we see the world. "When I am a reporter," I say to Jonah, "I will fly around the world to get my stories."

"I thought you wanted to be a detective?"

"Quiet."

I whisper, "A reporter-type detective, I think."

Mr. Amadeo walks around the class. He asks us questions about countries on the map. Using his pointer, he taps some of us on the shoulder. We get to go to the front and find the place we're looking for. "France." Evelyn locates that. "Russia." Lucky Bessie. Her father is the teacher. He calls on her twice, and smiles. East

Germany. West Germany. Czechoslovakia. I get passed over for those. "The People's Republic of China," he says. None of our hands go up, not even mine. But he calls on me anyhow. A few of the boys, in the ties Jonah bought, laugh on my way up. He gives one a good shove. I locate China. Bessie claps when I take my seat.

"My father says if you can read a map you can always find your way home," I say to the class.

Bessie's father says he will remember that. Then he talks about mountains and oceans. The Great Wall. Jonah asks about monkeys. He heard China has "a hundred million" of them there. Of course we laugh. Mr. Amadeo sits on the desk, explaining. He mentions a rainy forest there, too. And finds it on the map.

Jonah waits until Bessie's father is at the blackboard writing down a multiplication problem, before he apologizes to me. The last of the money is burning a hole in his pocket and besides, he says, people like him better when he's got a little something extra to pass along to them.

"I like you just fine the way you are." I lean over to get a good look at Bessie. "Don't we?"

She stares at him. Then smiles. Before picking up her pencil and writing right there on the nice clean desk in her father's classroom. *Yes.*

Jonah rears back and puffs up. With his hand raised high, he asks Mr. Amadeo if he could wipe and wash the boards clean at the end of the day. And do any running to the office or anyplace else he'd like. They will talk about it later, Bessie's father says. "Now for our times tables."

It's not long before we are dismissed for lunch. Everyone walks out of the building heading home to eat. I am on my way to the bank. Jonah also. His mother is away at his great-grandmother's house across town. Sick. I would not want Jonah to be alone so I invited him along. He might as well know what it takes to be a good businessman.

32

NO ROOM AT THE BANK

"Gal!" The secretary at the front desk stands up. "Get."
She points at the door. "I have told you once. Told you
twice. Haven't I? Uppity little thang. Now scat."

Jonah is backing up. Asking if my ears are filled with
wax. "She said leave, Octobia May. We gotta."

With a straight back, I spell out Auntie's name. "S-h-
u-m-a." Then her last name. "C-o-t-t-i-n-g-h-a-m.
She must be here." Stretching my neck, I look around.
"She said she would meet me. I can't leave until she
does." I fold my arms and shout. "Auntie!" The marble
floors of the bank make my voice echo. The tellers

standing in cages look away from their customers. A colored teller looks ashamed of me.

"Might I help you?" A lady with blue eyes in a black pencil skirt walks over to us, smiling. Her eyes are not so nice when they stare at Mrs. Anson. "Two little ones," she says, "in a big old bank by themselves. What may we do for you?"

With his hands looped through his suspenders, Jonah speaks up. "We got some business to take care of."

The lady at the front desk folds her pale arms. "I told them . . . both. The colored girls work at night cleaning up."

"Aunt Shuma's not a girl. She's all grown up." I turn and face the nice lady. "She told me to meet her here."

Mrs. Anson sits down at her desk. "How many times must I say it? Your aunt . . . isn't . . . here."

The nice lady clears her throat. She will handle things, she says. Mrs. Anson bites her bottom lip while she sharpens a No. 2 pencil. Then Jonah butts in. "Y'all giving her aunt a lotta money today."

"Oh, are we?" The lady holds up Mrs. Anson's candy jar and offers us peppermint. "Well, who is your aunt meeting with, sweetie?"

I stand up straight. "The president."

It's disrespectful to involve the bank president in our little game, she lets us know. "Moreover he is out of the office now, on business." Then her voice turns nice again. "I wish I could help you two, honestly I do."

She is talking to us while moving through the revolving doors. "Get along and find another game to occupy yourselves with." Outside in the sun, she pats her long, pretty hair and then steps back inside.

On the sidewalk. I hold on to Jonah's hand, wondering what I should do. *Maybe she didn't check the president's calendar carefully*, I think, walking back inside. Just as quickly, I'm on the sidewalk again.

It's Jonah's idea to find another way in. On the mystery radio shows there's always a trick drawer or side door, he reminds me. In the back, we only see a parking lot. But then I notice a gray, dented door with a fat knob. Inside, the steps lead down instead of up. They take us to a hall that leads to another hall and to three doors that will not budge.

When a brown wooden door creaks, then swings out wide, we duck behind a file cabinet and listen. Mr. Davenport and a man are talking. Next, I hear a woman's voice: Auntie. Suddenly, a man steps into the hall and walks back and forth for a while. We recognize him right away — from Sixth Street. When he opens the door to go back inside, we make our move. Pushing past him. Racing inside. We find what we've been looking for.

"Auntie!"

Mr. Davenport jumps up from the table. "What the dickens?"

"Hush. Come. Sit." Auntie holds tight to her pocketbook.

I squeeze behind the table and sit as close to her as I can. Jonah is beside me, practically in my lap.

"No one was to have a clue about our meeting." The banker frowns at Mr. Davenport. "That is why I had the two of you meet me in the storage room. I knew . . ." He talks about the reasons he wanted to meet with them after dark. Mr. Davenport wouldn't go along with his plans.

"Now" — the man holds his head and sighs — "it's all falling apart. I'll be in jail. I know it."

33

MR. DAVENPORT ALMOST
GETS HIS WAY

Mr. Davenport reminds me of the bad guys in the movies. His eyes squint and shift. His tight fist hits his other hand when he tries to make a point. *He is in charge*, I think, *not the banker.*

The banker is nervous. Walking back and forth across the room, he holds his hands behind his back. His fingers fight with his thumbs. Up and down they go, rubbing knuckles and scratching nails.

I don't think I've ever seen a nervous white man before. Not one afraid of Negroes anyhow. Mr. Harrison is scared of Mr. Davenport, that's easy to see. He does what he tells him to do, like sit down in the thick, dog-eared banker's chair at the head of the table. Take papers out of his briefcase. Place them in front of Auntie. "And shut up."

Auntie is never nervous. She is strong and brave and sure most every time. But not now. Under the table her leg is a pogo stick going up and down, up and down. The banker's voice is thin and soft like tissue. Mr. Davenport's voice shouts even when it's low and tight. I am quiet as I can be. But inside, I am giving him a piece of my mind.

Mr. Harrison sits an inkwell and pen on the table. He should never have contacted Mr. Davenport, he says. Never told him to come to town. "This is all your fault."

Mr. Davenport pulls the banker up by his black suit jacket. Gives him a good hard shake and turns him loose. The banker almost falls onto the floor on his way down. Auntie tries to steady him, before putting her warm arms around Jonah and me.

Mr. Harrison says his bank does not lend money to single women. And rarely to Negroes before he came. But he is a man who believes in helping people in need, he says, handing Jonah and me pieces of butterscotch candy. Just the kind of candy Mrs. Loewenthal likes.

I ask if Mr. Harrison lost anyone in the war like Mrs. Loewenthal did. Mr. Davenport spits across a pile of papers on the desk, into a dented spittoon, before he says we're running out of time. I bring up the soldiers Aunt Shuma and I saw at the post office the other day. She and I shook their hands.

I ask Mr. Davenport and Mr. Harrison if they ever went to war together. Fighting side by side. Auntie explains that during most of World War II, Negro troops had to bunk, eat, and serve in the war with their own kind. "But the men in charge of the troops — sergeants and generals and all that — well, they was almost always white, no matter the color of the troops. It's different now," she says. "Better."

Mr. Harrison's face turns red.

Mr. Davenport raises his voice. "A history lesson. Huh, Shuma? In the middle of the most important business transaction you will ever be involved in." He turns the pages of her contract until he gets to the very last one. He takes his hand and grabs my chin. "She does not know her place." I am a snoop, a busybody, a grown woman parading around in a child's body. A Negro girl who is being raised to think the world will treat me as Auntie does, he says. "Like you are as privileged and free as the men who run Wall Street."

"Where's Wall Street?" I whisper.

Auntie pleads with me to be quiet. "Our future is about to be put in my hands, child." She takes off her gloves, sitting her pillbox hat on the table beside her.

I look at Mr. Davenport and wonder about the money and jewels Jonah and I took. He never missed them. Maybe because there's plenty more where that came from.

Auntie stutters when she talks about the money she's got saved in the bank. "I'm good for whatever I borrow." She blinks and thanks Mr. Harrison for his kindness. "You gonna change everything in my life, by lending me this."

I keep my eye on Mr. Davenport. He keeps his eyes on me and Jonah. Sometimes he corrects Mr. Harrison, who tries to explain things to Auntie.

Reading the papers, she says, "I told you the amount I needed. You got more than twice that amount here." Auntie swallows, saying she could never repay what's written down.

Mr. Harrison explains more than once how helpful he is trying to be to Auntie. That when it comes to Negroes and women and rules at banks, well, things aren't fair. "I am trying to be fair, but, well, I have to get a little something in return . . . you know."

Mr. Davenport takes over the explaining. Auntie will get the amount she asked for. But they must ask for more than she needs because things just may one day get Mr. Harrison in trouble, so the extra is for the risk he is taking.

Mr. Davenport adds more to the story. Auntie cannot get the money in her name because, well, she is a spinster. So they will put her down as a Mrs. Johnson. And he will become Mr. Johnson — "on paper, of course." Since he is taking a risk as well, his amount is "reflected in the loan amount, too."

Forty thousand dollars is a lot of money, even I know that. "Don't sign, Auntie."

"It's a trick." Jonah wiggles.

"Who gonna lend a colored woman that much money — married or not?" Auntie snaps open her purse and takes out a picture. Of the building she wants to buy. Then out comes a piece of paper. There are rows of numbers and lots of questions written on it. I hear words like *interest rate*, *mortgage*, and *principal*. I whisper. She tries to explain what the words mean, but the banker and Mr. Davenport get upset with her. They should be done by now. She is wasting everyone's time, they say, needling her. Living alone, being independent for so many years has ruined her, they think. "Let us settle the matter for you and go home," Mr. Harrison insists.

I think about what all the grown-ups at our house want. For me to be a good girl and watch how I use my freedom. But I jump to my feet anyhow, nearly making it around the desk. "Leave her alone. She could be married if she wanted. And she doesn't want your old money!"

Jonah claps. Mr. Davenport loosens his tie. "One more word, Octobia May, and your aunt won't get a red cent."

"Please, child." Auntie yanks my arm when I am near her again, and makes me take my seat. "Let me chew on this."

While she ponders, I look around. At the floor. The ceiling. The two of them. First Mr. Davenport. Then Mr. Harrison. Back to Mr. Davenport. Again to Mr. Harrison, noticing for the first time his eyes. Wide apart, with a cut over the left one.

Auntie picks up a pen. Dipping the tip into ink, she writes her name. Her letters leap and loop and shout. *Miss Shuma May Cottingham.*

34

AUNTIE'S LOST DREAM

"Octobia May."

"Hush," I say to Jonah.

"But, Octobia May."

Auntie cuts her eyes at us. Walking with Jonah over to the window, I stare at the boats sailing along Bend River. His hands go around my ear, when he tells me he remembers where he first saw Mr. Harrison. "I know. I was there. Sixth Street," I remind him.

No, he says. Mr. Harrison needed extra help for a party he was having at his house. Jonah went there with his mother to empty the ashtrays and wipe up spills. She and his dad earn extra money doing things like that.

Walking over to our seats, Jonah stands beside the bank president. "Don't you remember me, Mr. Harrison?" he asks. "You patted my head and gave me chocolate at your house once."

I walk up to Mr. Davenport. "He robs banks, Auntie. Maybe they rob them together."

Mr. Davenport's hand goes high in the air, ready to slap me.

Auntie stands. She is a tall tree that will not bend when he threatens me. "Don't you dare!"

Jonah points to the bank president. "You killed your colored help, didn't you?"

Auntie looks them both over, like she is seeing them for the first time. I am standing beside her when she grabs for the papers. Mr. Davenport wrestles them from her. When I hit him with her purse, she throws ink on the papers, ruining them. "Octobia May. Don't you worry. He'll be moving out my place today for sure."

Jonah and I are close behind her, when Mr. Davenport takes a step to block the way. Auntie lifts the spittoon from the floor. "Don't think I won't."

Throwing a chair at the wall, he swears. "The day I met you was the second-worst day of my life." He is looking at me.

Outside the bank, Auntie looks sad enough to cry.

Stopping in front of Silverman's appliance store, Jonah wraps his arms around her belly. "Miss Shuma.

Don't cry. One day I will make enough money to lend to you."

"I'm sorry, Auntie. It was all my fault."

"I was so close. Had more freedom at my fingertips than ever before." Staring through the window at all those smiling, happy people on TV, Auntie weeps.

35

MR. DAVENPORT'S LAST DAY

Auntie throws another suitcase onto the porch. Mr.
Buster hauls a steamer trunk down the steps, sitting
it at the curb like Thursday's trash. "Well. Here he
come." Mr. Buster spits. "Wish I was the type to carry
a pistol."

Everyone is outside in rockers, waiting on trouble.
Mrs. Loewenthal is holding a heavy metal iron we use
to hold the back porch door open. Mr. Piers is peeling
a pear with a butcher knife. Miss Marble rocks, then
stops to pick her teeth with her knitting needle. She
wanted to bring out a cast-iron skillet, but her arthritis
is pestering her so.

Handmade silk shirts. Both straw and fine hats. The bare mattress he slept on. Even his typewriter filled with paper. All sit outside for the world to see. I ask about the bucket of sand. Mr. Buster pulls American flags from his back pocket. "He's no patriot, even if he love the flag. And I don't carry folks' beach souvenirs." He hands a flag to everyone who wants it.

Whistling, Mr. Davenport strolls toward our house like a man with no worries. Not even his things make the smile on his face disappear. Until he sees Auntie. "That big mouth of yours will get you and that niece of yours into trouble, if you do not keep it shut."

Aunt Shuma didn't tell our boarders everything that happened at the bank. "It's too dangerous," she told me. "And it ain't normal for Negroes to stand up to white folks like Mr. Davenport did; even up north." She said the hold that he has on the bank president is as powerful as voodoo. She does not want me, or Jonah's family, ending up in Bend River, so not one of us is to murmur a word.

Walking across the street to our place, Bessie stands beside me. Mr. Davenport picks over his things. Telling Auntie I may keep the typewriter, and use it to "keep that imagination of hers well-oiled and fueled."

I do not want it. Auntie does. She tells him it is the only decent thing he has done since he came here except to pay his rent in advance. Taking out her wallet, she hands him five dollars in singles, then takes the typewriter. Mr. Davenport stuffs the money into his jacket pocket.

"I'm not afraid of you." I stand closer to him. "And I'll find out what you and that bank president did to that lady."

"Octobia May!" Auntie holds on to the typewriter, looking afraid. "Please."

Mr. Buster asks the three of us to sit down on the porch. On his way to the pavement, he asks to speak to Mr. Davenport for a second. He is close to his ear, holding tight to his elbow even when Mr. Davenport tries to pull away. None of us hear what is being said, until Mr. Davenport begins to shout. "So what if you were in two wars? And can finish a man with your bare hands? I saw combat. At the Battle of the Bulge — plus."

Mrs. Loewenthal sets the iron down. "You . . . witnessed the massacre?

"Wereth?" His eyes dart back and forth. Landing for a while on Bessie.

"Malmédy."

Holding up his hands, he stares down at the porch. "No. I've seen the worst in men, nonetheless. So your threats — none of them — matters one iota to me, Buster."

Mrs. Loewenthal's voice gets as soft as a butterfly's wing. "You were there in Belgium, right? How awful for you."

Mr. Piers waves his flag. "How many died there that year, at the Battle of the Bulge? Trying to remember. So many died."

Mrs. Loewenthal and Mrs. Ruby hold hands. "I believe . . . more than eighty thousand American casualties. I read. Kept track. Every day of the war for years. The Russians. Americans. French. Canadians. The whole world fighting for us."

Mr. Davenport lets out a breath. "You don't forget what happens in war." He walks onto the porch. Looking at Mrs. Loewenthal, he says, "Or sleep easy ever again."

Mrs. Loewenthal pats her hands. "Thank you. Thank you for all your sacrifice. And you as well, Buster."

"Well, I'll be." Mr. Piers puts a bit of pear in his mouth. "Shuma had you pegged right from the start. I call you a hero."

Mr. Davenport likes Bessie's hair, I think. He stands staring at her a long while. When he walks into the house, Auntie does not stop him.

I tug on Mr. Buster's yellow shirt. "I think maybe Mr. Davenport used to be a true hero. But what made him change?"

Mr. Buster takes me into his arms. "War can change a man, sweetie. Grenades. Bombs. Boys washing up dead on the beach." Carrying me inside, he tries to change the subject, asking what kinds of stories I will type on my new machine.

"I can't use it," I say, accepting the cookie Mr. Piers offers me. "He's not a vampire. But — he's still not a very nice man."

Mr. Buster sits me down. "Well, then, maybe it's high time some nice people fiddled around with them keys." He winks.

One by one everyone else comes inside the house.

"We all owe you an apology, Octobia May." Mr. Buster sits underneath the window, pulling out his pipe. He says I saw something wrong in that man right from the start. And even though they are proud he served our country and risked his life, it does not excuse his present behavior. "Children got a second sense. That's what I say."

Auntie walks over to the secretariat and takes typing paper out of the drawer.

"Aunt Shuma, where did you get this?"

She is standing beside Mr. Buster, fanning herself with the paper. As soon as Mr. Davenport came to live in our house, she tells me, she put a typewriter on lay-away at the pawnshop. They gave her the paper for free. "I figured," she says, "the world got room for one more colored writer at least."

They are all around me, listening to me talk about the stories I plan to write, until Mr. Davenport finally comes downstairs. Taking his time, he walks over to me. "Where is it?"

I think about the money still in the furnace. But he is talking about the picture — of him and his friends. The tie clip, too. "I do not have them. And who would want them?" I say. Mr. Buster stands beside me insisting that Mr. Davenport leave, or else.

Mr. Davenport pauses for a while. "What's it matter? I don't even recognize those boys anymore."

Bessie stares.

The old Mr. Davenport returns. The one that can be as mean as a rattlesnake. Kneeling down, he pinches Bessie's cheek. And laughs. "Negro today. White tomorrow —"

"Mr. Davenport!" Auntie runs and swings the door open wide. "Get out of my house! Before I throw you out myself."

He keeps talking. "It's as easy as passing from one train to the next, little girl. I know. I do."

Carrying his bucket of sand, he leaves. That's when the grown-ups surround Bessie, asking if she's okay.

At the window, I watch to make sure he does not try to sneak back. That's when I see it. A truck with the electric company's name on it. Stopped at our streetlamp, a man pulls out a long ladder. I ask what he is up to. He answers only when Aunt Shuma asks the very same question. Soon, he says, we will have electric lighting on our street, too. After a while the whole block comes outside. Sitting on porches. Sipping tea. Rocking. Calling across the street to one another, everyone is excited. But nobody is as excited as I am. I got two big surprises today. Mr. Davenport is gone forever. And our street is changing for the better, bit by bit.

36

MAKING NEW PLANS WITH JONAH

"Jonah!"

"Quiet, child."

"Come down here!"

"Octobia May. Silence." Jonah's mother sits in their first-floor window using binoculars to watch the television in the house across the street. "Reading lips is hard enough without you causing a scene."

In the summer and early fall, Jonah sleeps outside on the third-floor landing. I can see his mattress and blanket from here. "Did you hear?" I ask his mother.

"Hush."

"Mr. Davenport moved out of our house a few days ago."

Mrs. Nicholson does not move her eyes. "Where to?"

"I don't —"

"He leave a forwarding address? My niece still rearing to meet him. Gotta speak to Shuma about things." I am on the second-floor landing, and she still hasn't told me to get away from her house yet. Jonah must be right. Television hypnotizes her.

Jonah has important news for me, too, he says once I get upstairs. His mother and father are going to the bank president's house in a few weeks. He is having a big party. He'll need plenty of help, so Jonah's working there, too.

Sitting on the mattress, I tell Jonah that I will be going also. The banker and Mr. Davenport are up to something. I plan to find out what it is.

Jonah shakes his head no. "My mother don't believe in a person tagging along unless she invites 'em. And she would never ask you to go anywhere, Octobia May."

I mention Mr. Davenport being a war hero and a bad guy both at the same time. "Can't you see, Jonah? The secret of Mr. Davenport gets bigger every minute. If we solve it, and I write the story, we will be famous," I tell him. "Don't you want to be famous, Jonah? More important than all the boys in the world — colored or white?"

Jonah gives my short little pigtail a good pull. "Oh, Octobia May. I can already feel the whipping I'm gonna get." Standing at the railing, he rubs his backside. Whistling, he talks about the bank president's house. It is far away. With so many floors they don't even use some. Jonah turns to face me. "What's the dead colored help have to do with all of this war stuff anyway?" he wonders.

I'm not sure. "Maybe nothing. Maybe everything," I say.

He stands at the railing squinting at the TV across the street for a while. "What if more colored help is dead on his property, Octobia May? Buried in the shed. Floating faceup in the bathtub on the fourth floor."

Jonah has a plan this time, he tells me. Like he was thinking it up all morning long. I kiss him on the cheek for his good idea.

"Well, you little hussy." His mother sticks her head out his bedroom window. "Wait until I tell your aunt."

Scurrying down the fire escape, jumping over the last three steps, I get away as fast as I can.

"You're a disgrace, Octobia May! To all girls. And keep yourself away from my boy!"

Looking over my shoulder, I bump into the mailman. Knocking pieces of mail out of his hand. "Sorry, mister." I round the corner, bumping into an old lady's shopping cart. Baked beans. A small brown bag of sugar.

Spam. Falling out of her cart, rolling across the pavement and into the street. "I'll pick it up. I didn't mean —" Sitting her things back in her cart, I make my way up the street.

Walking beside Bend River, I imagine what the bank president's house must look like. And how Jonah and I will capture him and Mr. Davenport and hold them for the police. Whistling and carrying a big stick, I tap the ground and skip. People smile and look at me with question marks in their eyes. Some even warn me. "Get home, little girl. It's getting too late to be by this river. In this fall air."

I say good evening and smile and think about what Mrs. Ruby told me earlier. Freedom gives you choices. That is why it's so good to be free. Thinking harder on it, enjoying my freedom, I sit and watch the river dance. But then I see him — Mr. Davenport. Not too far away.

37

AUNT SHUMA AND THE LONG ARM OF THE LAW

He is prancing up the street as bold as the day is long. Ducking behind a yellow Thunderbird, I keep my eyes on him. *Is he still living in our neighborhood?* I wonder. *Will he ever pick up his fancy suitcases and things?*

He turns the corner, flipping a coin. I stand up ready to follow him. "Got ya!" Pulling me by my ear, Officer O'Malley drags me over to the sidewalk. "He told me to be on the lookout for you. But I'd never expect you to be so easily found." He slaps his hand with his night-stick. "You'll likely be in jail soon enough, Octobia May, girl. Right along with your aunt. The thief."

"What did you do to Auntie?"

Mr. Davenport's no hero. He's a liar and a thief. Officer O'Malley would know that if he would just listen to me. But his finger goes to his lips, every time I break into his story. When Mr. Davenport returned to Auntie's and went to his room, he was looking for jewelry he'd forgotten, Officer O'Malley tells me. It was gone, so he says. "And where was it, by golly? In your aunt's room. Tucked away in her skirt pockets. Smart man, that one. He left it there for us to find." He never trusted her fully, he tells me. He takes off his hat and pats his forehead. "Without a man in the house, a woman might think herself capable of anything."

My legs try to give out from underneath me. I won't let them. I have to stay strong for Auntie. But right this minute, I wish I had on a dress. A fancy hat and gloves. Things like that make a better impression. "Officer O'Malley . . . Aunt Shuma would never steal." I sniffle. "Please don't make her stay in jail. Please." I think about the colored men on the chain gangs down south. They sing but something inside them is long gone, you can tell. "She makes you apple butter every year. Doesn't she?"

"That is not the point, girlie." Officer O'Malley walks me past the river, smiling at all the people who smile at him. He stopped her from pawning the jewelry or selling it to hoodlums, he believes. He thinks Mr. Davenport was charitable in giving Auntie a few days to turn her own self in. "It's no secret," he says, "that she's got grand ideas. Your neighbors and I chat. She plans to purchase more land, I hear."

The sun is bright and the river is calm, but inside I am scared. Officer O'Malley wants to know if my parents have a house phone. He will have his captain call them from the station and put me on the first train home. "You can't." I stop walking.

"What did you say to me?" He pulls me along.

He can't send me home. Who will save Auntie if I leave town? How will I prove that Mr. Davenport and the banker are doing bad things? "Officer O'Malley . . ."

A man walking toward us pushes his hat down. When he gets to the corner he stops and tips it.

My feet are brakes that keep me from moving. "Mr. Harrison," I whisper.

Officer O'Malley reminds me what happens to girls like me who trouble the world. Holding up his nightstick, he clears his throat. "Walk, child . . . or else."

I make a choice. Digging my teeth into Officer O'Malley's hand. Kicking him twice in the shins. Watching his leg buckle, I run.

Zigzagging past whites and coloreds trying to nab me because Officer O'Malley is telling them to, I turn the corner. Then another. Making a right. Another left. I watch Mr. Harrison disappear again.

Soon enough I see Officer O'Malley standing on the corner looking for me. I am hiding behind a car, peeking out now and then. Not far from the street where Mr. Davenport killed the lady in white.

38

BAD GUYS MAKING BAD PLANS

"She's in jail. You're sure about that?" Mr. Harrison puffs on a big, fat cigar. "Now . . . what about her niece? I just saw her. With that cop."

Mr. Davenport and Mr. Harrison are in the house. Listening outside the window, I try not to be discovered. Mr. Davenport doesn't want to talk about me. But he wouldn't worry, he says, Officer O'Malley will handle me. "He will have her on a train headed home before we know it." He asks for his money. He will leave town soon, he says. "Europe. To see how she is fairing."

The banker talks about Auntie and the application. That money was to be Mr. Davenport's, too. Finally I understand what they were doing at the bank. Auntie was never to get the money. It was for Mr. Davenport all along. Every cent. After she left, it turns out, they made a new application. Forging Auntie's signature, they said she was married to Mr. Davenport. And changed her *Miss* to *Mrs.* But now Mr. Davenport can't get the money, either. A vice president got his hands on the paperwork and said it looked fishy. The banker was out of the office. The man took the application to two people. "Couple this with the missing money I've given you, and they are pressuring me to call in the police."

"You run the blasted bank, don't you?"

"Yes, but —"

"Well, then, get me my money! All those dead bodies were bad enough. Now with Shuma in custody, colored or not, the police may begin to listen to her."

Mr. Harrison's ears turn red, and then his entire face follows. Pacing, he says he has decided not to give Mr. Davenport another dime. "You've made a sloppy mess of things, Hardy. You weren't even capable of handling a small child. Today I made up my mind — I'm done with it! I came to tell you that."

Putting his foot on the couch and a hanky in his hand, Mr. Davenport politely wipes his shoes. "They can't see too well at that bank, can they? But I can see —

everything. Where would you be if I talked? In jail, I believe." He walks over to a bottle of wine and pours himself a glass. "Or maybe on a chain gang down south. Bet Georgia's looking for a good old boy like you."

"Do not bring up Georgia!"

"Fine. I won't mention Macon."

"Chicago, either —"

"Or the army?" Mr. Davenport scratches his chin. "A black man passing . . ."

They argue for a while. Talking about a passing train. The Negro section. And he and Mr. Harrison during the war. "Jim Crow is a strange old bird," Mr. Davenport says. "Flew over there right along with us. But he wasn't any bother to you, now, was he?" He grits his teeth and stares into Mr. Harrison's gray-blue eyes. "You were free and easy the entire time, right, Sergeant?" He salutes before he socks the banker, who socks him back.

Furniture breaks. Bear sounds — grunts and growls — move around the room along with them. They end up under a table, rolling past the lit fireplace. Fists punching.

When everything is quiet, the banker stands up, holding his bloody ear. Wiping his bleeding nose. "Okay. Okay. I have more money at home. Twenty-five thousand or so. It's never good to invest your own money in things like this. But will that do?"

Mr. Davenport agrees.

"Just don't ruin my life." The banker says he's worked so hard for it. "If the military . . . people here in town . . . found out . . ."

Mr. Davenport shakes his head up and down.

"You know . . . you know. It would all be gone forever; and me too."

They both agree. Mr. Davenport will come to the banker's house during the party. While everyone is having a good time, they will meet in the banker's library and take the money from his vault. Once Mr. Davenport's gone, Mr. Harrison'll report the missing money to the police. "Bring the jewels with you. Especially that ring. If my wife —"

"Your wife wouldn't have the ring if it weren't for me. It was supposed to be for my wife. My daughter. If I had ever married." Mr. Davenport heads for the door. "What's it matter? I'm leaving town anyhow. Okay. At your house. Yes. During the party." He laughs. "All of you fancy folks hobnobbing for charity." He opens the door. "So I won't ever need charity, add an extra ten thousand to the pot. God knows I've earned it."

I can see in Mr. Harrison's eyes that he does not like Mr. Davenport much anymore. But he isn't complaining. He sits down in a chair, tending to the blood dripping on his white collar. That's when I make my getaway.

39

GRAVEYARD PLANS

It is black as tar when I walk through the graveyard, humming to keep myself company. Crying in between.

Stopping to visit the Before Girls, I sit down and pluck weeds. I do not have a home to go back to, I tell them. Auntie is in jail and crooks want me out of the way. But I am free, with two good hands, plenty enough to set things right in this world, as soon as I can think of what to do next.

"You never met Auntie," I say to the baby girl. "She wants to own lots of hotels and put my name on them."

Click.

I think of Bessie. If only I had her camera tonight. Or she was here in the graveyard keeping me company.

I make my way over to Juppie. Mr. Alexander will not like it, but I will sleep here tonight. "A lullaby for you, Juppie." Singing softly, I lay down beside her headstone. "Come back, girl. I need you," I say, drifting off.

"Octobia May."

Jonah is calling for me. "If you can hear me, say something."

It takes me a while to make my way over to him. Holding a flashlight, he shines it bright in my face. "The police are looking for you."

"I know."

He kicks at autumn leaves on the ground. "Your aunt's in jail and . . . You can't bite the police, Octobia May."

"I know."

They say I almost took Officer O'Malley's finger off. "You're colored, Octobia May. When you gonna realize that?" He lowers his voice, telling me that Auntie's boarders have been looking for me as well. He points left. Mr. Buster is in that direction. He turns and points right. Mr. Piers and Mrs. Loewenthal are near the fence. "Them old people should be in bed. But they out here, worrying over you."

Mrs. Nicholson is here, too, because she says the law comes down awful mighty hard on colored folks, Jonah lets me know. "And even though she don't care for you much, she don't want to see all the bad that could happen to you once the law steps in."

Mr. Buster is yelling my name for a while. My hand is covering Jonah's mouth to keep him from giving me away. Pulling him under a tree, I let him know, "They'll send me home. I can't save Aunt Shuma if I'm sitting on the porch with my mother standing over me."

Jonah pushes away my hand and tries to break free. "Come home with me."

"No!"

His mother does not have to know, he tells me. He surprises me when he says she and those Do Some Good women want to do good by Auntie and bring her food in jail. He smiles. "I think they like her some, even if she don't have a husband." Jonah said that all evening those ladies were in Auntie's kitchen cooking for our boarders.

"Come." He takes me by the hand. "Here." I did not smell it at first, but he has two big pieces of garlic with him. "I will even peel 'em for you." Jonah thinks they will remind me some of Auntie's place.

I eat them one by one, and promise I will stay with him. But we can't let his mother or Mr. Buster know that I'm here. When we hear them coming our way, Jonah hurries me along. Trying to lead me out of the graveyard. I stop where the soldiers lie and salute. The flags on the graves make me think of the ones that came out of Mr. Davenport's room. When this is all over, I will start planting flags, too.

"Hurry up, Octobia May. We need a plan — a place to hide you."

Kneeling, I lift one of the flags up like a plucked flower. "Oh, Jonah. He did this. Mr. Davenport put these flags here." I know it deep in my soul.

"But why?"

I pull out the picture and look at the little boy without the tie. "I don't know."

But we do not have time to figure it out now. And I cannot go to his house just yet, I say, smelling to high heaven like a garlic tree. I lead Jonah to Mr. Davenport's old mausoleum. I will hide there until everyone gets tired and makes their way home. Jonah hands me a flashlight and his one and only true Satchel Paige baseball card. "To keep you company," he says, running off.

When it is almost morning, I go to Jonah's place. As easy as night slides into day, I climb up the fire escape. We have it all planned out. I will stay with him at night. During the day I will hide in the graveyard. I will miss a lot of school. But what does it matter, if Auntie is missing her freedom?

40

HIDING OUT AT JONAH'S PLACE

"I never slept outside under the stars before, Jonah."

"Ain't it nice?"

"Look. The North Star."

"Is it really?"

"I like to pretend that I know where it is. If the Before Girls were alive they would show me." I tell Jonah a secret. I cannot hear them talk much anymore. My pretend servant friends, either. It is like they are fading away like shooting stars.

Jonah is beside me. "Sometimes out here I pretend

my crooked eye is as handsome and bright as a star. Do you think I'm handsome, Octobia May?"

We each lay in blankets, with our feet on the railings. "I do, Jonah." I make a wish for Auntie to stay cheerful and clean while she is locked away. Yawning, I close my eyes tight. "Funny, Jonah, how you don't worry about some things when big things step into your life."

"Like what?"

"My hair. I haven't thought about it once since Auntie went to jail last week."

"I been thinking, Octobia May. Short hair on a girl might just look better anyway."

"Just might." I close my eyes. "Huh, Bessie?"

Jonah says we will all be in trouble soon enough. Because I was so sad, he made a pact with Bessie. After her folks went to sleep, he would come by for her. She was sitting on the porch when he showed up. He will get her back in the morning before anyone suspects, he says.

Bessie takes out a picture of me and Auntie. We are sitting on the porch. She is oiling my hair. I am laying on her lap, happy. "Thank you, Bessie." She holds one of my hands while Jonah holds the other. "I wish you had your camera right now," I say, yawning. "We could take a picture of everything. That big old moon. Us three. Even the fire-escape steps." With Auntie in jail, I tell them, I've learned that things can change sooner than you think.

"I know," Bessie says.

Jonah sits up lickety-split. "Octobia May —"

"I heard, Jonah." I ask her to talk some more. She stares. Then smiles when she pulls more pictures out of her pocket.

It is my third night sleeping at Jonah's place, but tonight is the most special one of all. Bessie talked. And she'll say more day by day, I know it.

The chill of the night doesn't bother me one bit. But after they go to sleep, I do feel a little sad. I am thinking of Auntie. My birthday is at the end of the month. What if she's in jail still? How long can I hide out and miss school without my parents rushing up and stealing me away? Freedom. "I got all I can handle and more now, Auntie. But it's not the same without you." I whisper, "I love you," and ask the stars to carry my words safe and sound over to her.

Then I nudge Bessie. "Please say one more word," I ask. I am nearly asleep when she answers. "My name is Bessie Amadeo. My best friend is Octobia May. It used to be my older brother, Larry."

41

MRS. NICHOLSON HAS A CHANGE OF HEART

"I knew it!" Jonah's mother reaches through the window, trying to catch me.

Bessie takes off down the fire escape, running past the iceman's truck.

"Please, Momma. Don't send Octobia May away."

I am on my knees when I beg Mrs. Nicholson not to send me home. Holding on to the window ledge, Jonah's mother orders him to come inside. With her mouth set as tight as the skin on a Chinese apple, she orders me to do the same. Jonah comes up with all manner of stories to get her to let me stay. Mr. Davenport might kill me, he says. "That is, if the police don't throw her in jail first." What about my hair? He's pulling at it like loose leaves. "It's a sight. Do you want white folks thinking all coloreds look this way?"

Mrs. Nicholson's hands go to her hips while she looks over my head. Mumbling, she brings up Auntie. She asked her to tend to me while she's away. Looking sleepy, Jonah's mother brings up the time I cut my hair. "Embarrassing all the Negroes in town." But she's onto Jonah's trick. Soon she's back to me leaving their place. She had planned to invite me to stay before I pulled this trick on her. "Get a nickel from your father, Jonah. We'll call her people in Pittsburgh and . . ."

I follow behind his mother. "I can't leave," I tell her. "Or I will never see Auntie again."

Her finger wags. Grown-ups run this house, she reminds me. They make the rules. Children follow along.

Jonah leaves the room to get the nickel. I sit on the velvet couch, thinking. I can match wits with any grown-up, I'm sure about that. But when it comes to Jonah's mother, it's terribly hard to win.

When my stomach growls and churns, Mrs. Nicholson leads me into the kitchen. Sitting out bread and butter, she tells me to have my fill. "You brought the cops to my house twice now." The first time was when Jonah and me found Mr. Davenport in the graveyard. Yesterday was the other time, I learn.

Jonah comes back with the nickel. He must get to the phone booth right away, since it's late. He is to call from the phone on my block, she tells him, and ask whoever answers to put Mr. Buster on the line. She wants him to phone my parents and have them come for me. Jonah starts to leave the room. Almost in the hall, he stops and comes back.

"Couldn't she use some right home training, Mom?" He flops on the plastic couch cushions. He repeats what she told him about Auntie not being fit to raise a girl. He says he knows she can do better by me if she gives herself half a chance.

His mother has always looked at me like a pesky fly she would be happy to smash. Right now her eyes seem different. Walking all around me. Looking me over from shoestring to crown. She squints. "We wear dresses in this house, Octobia May." She tells Jonah to get moving. He has to go to my place and get clothes from Mr. Buster. "No pants," she shouts. "They turn a gal restless."

Mrs. Nicholson does not like hugs, I think. With me squeezing her hard she keeps her arms stiff as the planks on the pier. "Oh. My hair? Auntie plaits it every day."

She digs and pocks around my scalp. "Goodness gracious." She's circling me. "Ain't gonna tackle this every day, no matter how short it is. Might just have to give you that perm you've been wanting. The right way, that is."

Standing still. Trying to hold back tears. I thank her. Me with my hair permed. I can see it clear as day. Only it doesn't seem right going against Auntie's rules now, when she can't send me to get switches for breaking them. Or share in my sorrow if it all goes wrong again. With my voice low, I share my thoughts with Mrs. Nicholson. Heading for the icebox, she walks back with jelly jars in her arms. "Didn't want this. But your aunt insisted. Go to her place and get several jars for my family. That's what I was told." Smiling at me, she says with all the Do Some Good ladies present, Auntie asked her especially to look after me. "Shuma said you'd turn wild as the wind without a strong woman to steer you straight." Quietly she apologizes for almost breaking her promise a bit earlier.

This time when I hug her, she gives me a tight squeeze back. Officer O'Malley trusts her, she says, patting my head. When someone is up to tomfoolery in our neighborhood, she is the one to whisper in his ear. She told him already that if I came around she would rush to the station and inform him. "Do not make me honor my word, child."

I ask her about school. She thinks a moment. What has to be done has to be done. In the morning she will take herself to the police station and give Officer O'Malley some news. "Ain't lying for you, child. But . . ." If she tells him that she heard I was shipped

back home, then she won't be lying. "It's what I heard."
Then he won't be looking for me anymore, she says.
While she is sure I will end up in a home for unruly
girls one day, it will not happen while I am living at her
place. "I mean that. And as for school, well, Jonah will
just have to share with you what he learns every day."

42

LEARNING TO LIVE WITHOUT AUNTIE

Mr. Buster had to come to see me, he says, hugging me. The rest of our boarders did, too. They pile into Mrs. Nicholson's house carrying canes and riding in wheelchairs. Mr. Piers walks up to me first. He will not apologize for crying, he lets everyone know. He thought I was shot and dead someplace, so these are happy tears, he promises. Mrs. Loewenthal went to her synagogue to talk to the rabbi about me. "He took your name to a private place," she says, "and the God who has no name brought you back to us." Kissing me, she tells me to stoop down. Taking a chain off her neck, she puts it on mine. It's the Star of David. "Now the one who never sleeps shall watch over you, too."

Miss Marble looks frail today. Skipping over to her, I give her a giant kiss on her wrinkled cheek. "Mrs. Nicholson," I ask when she brings coffee for everyone to drink, "can I have some, too?"

They all stare at her, waiting for her to make a giant fuss. She does. Complaining that a child should not have grown-up food or mature before her time. When she goes out of the room for peach cobbler and saucers, Mr. Buster waves me over. "Just a sip." He even blows the coffee before I drink.

"Have you seen Auntie?" I ask. "I want to visit her, but Jonah's mother says no."

Auntie does not want me to see her in jail, he says. If she is not out by next week, she will give him my mother's phone number. He will call my family to come to take me home. But then he lets me in on a secret. He has been following Mr. Davenport. "But I ain't no detective. He see me every time."

The ladies change the subject, telling me they are all on their way to visit Auntie. In the hearse Mr. Buster borrowed from work, there are newspapers, a picture of me, *Ebony* magazine, and some food for her to eat, they say. "Oh." Mr. Buster excuses himself for a minute. When he comes back in the house he is carrying Mr. Davenport's typewriter. "If you can write something nice and pretty for her, we will make sure she gets it."

At the dining room table, I slide in the typing paper. While I type, I hear Mrs. Nicholson talk about Auntie's shed. "A disaster. We will put that in order. Right after we clear out your closet, Octobia May."

I swallow. "My closet."

"A disgrace. You have more patched pants and thinned shirts than Jonah. Some of the ladies . . ." They have daughters my age and lots of hand-me-downs. They will fit me for a few things this evening, she tells me. While Auntie is gone they will also work with me on the way I walk and on how to keep my mouth closed while I eat. "And then . . ." I do not want to think of what else they want to do to me. "I want to talk to you about a few things. Like chasing grown men around town."

I open my mouth, but Mr. Buster interrupts my words. He says for me to hurry along so they can do their visiting with Auntie. I type one finger at a time, making a few mistakes.

Dear Aunt Shumaa,

I mis s you. How are you? I am fine. I wear a dres now everyday even on saturday. Jonah's mother does not have any daughters and i think she is taking it out on me. I do not mind it much be cause I get to stay here in the city close to you. I sleep on the sofa. His mother makes it up every Night for me. I want to sleep outside with Jonah, but she said not over her dead body. It's getting cooler everyday so he won't be out there long. That is the only thing that keeps me from saying any-thing. Oh, I heard one of the Do Some good ladies say you were very sad. when I visit, I will cheer you up.

Love Octobia May

P.S. I forgot to tell you. Mrs. Loewenthal knows somebody they call a ward leader, who eats with the man who in charge of all the police, who called officer O'Malley's captain and said that I am a nice little col-ored girl who should not be in with the juveniles so Officer O'Malley should not keep knocking on doors asking about me. I am happy about that. but when I ask Mrs. Loewenthal to help you, she said she could no. She tried. But stealing expensive jewelry is too big a thing for her friends to undo. I will undo things myself, Auntie, as fast as I can. Do not get discouraged.

Octobia May

43

TAKING OFFICER O'MALLEY
BY THE HAND

With Jonah's cap on my head, I tiptoe down the fire escape. And run. On the corner I put on shoes, and notice how the fog can swallow you up. I'm moving slowly. Taking two steps then stopping to see if I am heading in the right direction. Holding my hands out in front of me, making sure I don't walk into walls. Or end up in the river. I keep on with my big plan.

Footsteps are behind me after a while. I stop. They stop. Walking faster, I take the steps down to Bend River. And do not go my regular route.

Feet are close on my trail. I speed up. Boats blow their horns and show their bright lights, but cannot help me any. A woman walking toward me is carrying a little girl. "Excuse me, miss . . ." I try to get her attention. "Somebody is —"

She does not stop. "It ain't none of our business." Disappearing like the river, they pass by me and run up the steps.

I walk as fast as I can. "Got ya!" From behind, strong hands snatch me like grapes from a vine, and squeeze me so tight I cannot escape.

"Get off of me. Turn me a loose." I twist and turn, closing my eyes, I punch whoever is trying to kill me.

"Octobia May. Did you think I wouldn't catch up to you?"

"Officer O'Malley?"

He sets me down and stands facing me. "And who else would be out here by the river on a day like this, except civil servants or the strange in the head?"

He bends down to my height. "Can't you do what you've been told ever, girlie? What everyone in this city has been told to do?" He takes me by the arm. "Home with ya." He pulls me along.

"I can't . . ." I fix my feet on the ground as firm as cobblestones. "I'm going this way."

"No more of this, child. Your auntie —"

"You talked to Auntie? She won't let me visit. She told Mr. Buster she'd put everyone out if they brought me there." Auntie told them there are some things a child shouldn't witness: a foul-mouthed woman and a lady in jail. I ask him why the police won't let her come home.

"Leave that to the officers of the law, Octobia May. We know a few things."

The fog and cold give me a chill. Officer O'Malley takes off his coat and puts it over my shoulders. "A colored girl biting a cop. It's enough to get you locked up, you know."

I've been keeping up my reading of the newspaper lately, for Auntie's sake. And noticing that *Negro* is the word the newspaper uses most. So I tell him to call me that from now on.

Even in the fog, I see Officer O'Malley's face turn red. "Negro. Colored. It's no matter to me. If you bite me one more . . ."

I look up into his eyes and blink. He shakes his head and says he'd better get me home. I tell him I have something to show him. He isn't listening. He is walking away, whistling and holding tight to my hand. I mention the bank president. He is pulling me along like a pup on a leash. I bring up Clinton Avenue, the grand party, stolen jewels, how they forged Auntie's signature.

"You've pestered poor Mr. Davenport day and night

while he was under your Auntie's roof. Now he's gone. Free. And your agitation continues."

He warns me that he'll have no more of my nonsense. I will mind my manners and be the nice colored Negro girl my aunt is trying to raise me into. He's mumbling to himself about meeting with his captain to discuss changing beats. I ask him to turn my hand loose so I may tie my shoestrings.

"No, lassie. You tricked me with that last time. A second bite, and you'll be on a chain gang for sure, I'll tell you that."

"Do they put children on chain gangs, Officer O'Malley?" I say as he drags me along. "Mr. Buster's brother was on one once. He said it is absolutely terrible."

"That it is, child."

"Is it just for coloreds? I mean Negroes?" Talking about it makes me wonder if that will happen to Auntie.

"Mostly," he says. "Some whites. Sometimes." He coughs. "But . . ." We both listen to the foghorn blow low and sad, like it could cry. "Do you always have to trouble a body, Octobia May? Can't you just be a quiet little girl?"

"If I was on a chain gang?"

"Bloody day in the morning."

"I would break those chains and free everybody." Skipping along, I say, "I think all people should be free. Don't you, Officer O'Malley?"

"How did I deserve the likes of you, child?"

I mention Mr. Davenport and Mr. Harrison again, but he forbids me to say either of their names once more tonight. I think I am being polite when I ask, "Do you like having red hair?"

He likes it just fine, he says, telling me to quit my talking. I ask if he knows that Negro people don't have red hair very often. "Except my cousin. She has red hair. And red eyebrows. And . . ."

Pulling me along. Asking why I can't keep my eyes ahead of me instead of behind, he wonders out loud. "How'd a colored man get to be so high-minded anyhow?" He stops. "That Mr. Davenport. So — fancy. Suits and fine hats. Luggage the best I've ever seen. And he leaves it at the curb like garbage." He says that has worried him since the day Mr. Davenport left Auntie's house. "But you, child, befuddle me so I forget the details of life."

My father wears sophisticated suits. He is a professor, but they won't let him teach at the university so he teaches at a high school and cleans office buildings at night. I tell Officer O'Malley about my father. He is quiet again. "Octobia May," he says, when we are crossing another street. "Would you know that house on Clinton again if you saw it once more?"

"Yes! I'll take you there right now."

"Then do it, child," he says, letting go of my hand.

44

GOOD-BYE, OFFICER O'MALLEY

Clinton Avenue makes Officer O'Malley and I both shiver. The fog clouds all of the houses and the cold makes his hands feel like they're dead. He wants me to stay back while he investigates the house. "I have to come along because I do not know the address," I tell him, returning his jacket to him. He talks to me about the importance of being quiet. But he is the one with the noisy shoes and loud whispers. Step by step. House after house. He holds my fingers tighter. I point at the house where I saw them last.

"Stay here," he says.

Officer O'Malley is quiet for a moment. Staring across the street at the house, he licks his lips and rubs his stubby chin. "I'll need to look around a bit.".

"Officer O'Malley . . ."

"Yes, child?"

"Do you ever wear suits?"

It takes him a while to answer. "Only to church, child. To stand before the Lord and Blessed Mother Mary." When he begins to cross the street, the fog swallows him up.

"I can't see you."

"Hush."

"But I want to come."

"Stay back, girlie," he whispers. "I mean it. Or you'll find the devil kinder than me."

I stand in the fog for a long while. Finally I cross the street, heading toward the back of the house. They have the curtains closed, but I can see inside a little. On the floor with blood running out of his mouth, I see Officer O'Malley.

The dead still cry on Clinton Avenue. I wonder if Officer O'Malley is crying, too. Laying on the floor with Mr. Davenport standing over him. His eyes are closed. Blood is leaking onto the floor from where they hit him in the head. Mr. Davenport checks his breathing.

"I . . . I killed him." Mr. Harrison steps aside.

"We'll let the river take care of him," Mr. Davenport says.

I hold my mouth to keep my screams inside.

"It was a mistake. I didn't mean —"

"I know. You never mean anything by the things you do." He leaves the room and comes back with a blue blanket. "Like the train ride from Georgia."

"Not Georgia again."

"I told you to meet me on the train." They wrap the body in the blanket. "I was running late. Cutting it close."

"Hardy. We were boys. Fifteen and thirteen. Runaways."

Mr. Davenport wipes blood off the nightstick. "I knew my place. I sat in the colored section."

The banker takes rope and wraps it around Officer O'Malley. He saw his chance, he says, so he took it. They pull the ends of the rope tight. "The conductor called me a well-groomed, God-fearing Protestant lad. He showed me where I belonged. Asked me where I was headed. 'Iowa.' He put that idea in my head, so I went. Took a seat. It felt right."

"Why didn't you say Chicago? Land of tenement houses. Sharecroppers running there for their lives. Oh. That's right. That was my lot. My fate. Never yours."

Mr. Davenport walks away wiping sweat off his brow. The banker reaches for the light. Turning it off, he says, "I was one hundred percent American. For once. Who wouldn't want that?"

"Yes, Harrison, who wouldn't want that." Mr. Davenport brings up his army days.

Why can't the grown-ups forget the war?

"Fort Dix, New Jersey, almost took the wind out of my sails. Serving my country, newly recruited, I was surprised to run into you." Mr. Davenport talks about Negro and white soldiers rioting at the movies. Mess halls. And other cities where there were riots; Negroes wrongly accused of mutiny. "But still fighting against Jim Crow."

The banker asks a question that Mr. Davenport does not have an answer for. "Wasn't it . . . a good idea to have me there? An officer with his own battalion. Looking out? Always, always putting my neck in a noose for the Negro soldier?"

It wasn't easy, he says. The other officers resented it. Reported him at times, too.

"Guilt makes a stone pillow, I suppose. So do not look to me to place feathers in it."

Mr. Harrison puts his arm over Mr. Davenport's shoulder. "In the end, we both helped to change the military. Change the South . . . the whole country."

"We? The Negro soldier did that. Not you."

Mr. Harrison turns the light off again and opens the door. "Don't say that. We need each other. We always have."

Together they drag the body outside.

45

MAKING FRONT-PAGE NEWS

Mrs. Nicholson drops the newspaper in my lap, reading the headline out loud. "Negro Girl Last Seen Talking to Missing Cop." She shakes her head and stares at Officer O'Malley's picture. The police say they don't know where he is. But I do. The dead come floating back to us lately.

Mrs. Nicholson uses her reading glasses to take a second look at the sketch the woman with the little girl gave the police. "Sakes alive! It . . . it's you, child."

Jonah agrees. "She's got your dimple, Octobia May." He lowers his voice. "And pretty eyes."

In the article they say the lady could not see the little girl very well. The description is of a girl wearing a navy-blue jacket. Mine was black. The girl had ribbons in her hair, the woman reported. Mrs. Nicholson does not believe in girls wearing ribbons. Only rag ties. Plus I wore a cap. But my small eyes and chin, plus my only dimple, she noticed those all right. In so much fog, I do not know how.

Someone bangs and bangs on the door, ringing the bell at the same time. "All right. Hold your pants up." Mrs. Nicholson shakes the newspaper at me. "Outta of my house. Just as soon as I get rid of whoever's trying to knock my door down."

I jump into Mr. Buster's arms, like a frog leaping out of hot water. He's seen the newspaper, he tells us. And recognized me right away. He asks what I know about all of this, but I do not say. It would only bring more trouble to Auntie's door.

Mrs. Nicholson sends Jonah to the store for a slab of fatback. Excusing herself, she leaves Mr. Buster and me alone. But not for long. Sitting my packed suitcase and the typewriter at the front door, she asks us both to leave. "You got something to do with poor Officer O'Malley being pitched into the river. I know it."

"Who saying he was in the river?" Mr. Buster asks. "Not the papers. Or the radio."

She swings open her front door, then closes it. "You a new kind of colored, child. Think you can do and be like the whites. Well, now we'll see how free you is with a dead Irish cop sitting at your feet." She will go to the police if she ever sees me with Jonah again, she warns. She will go to the police if I so much as say good day to her, she yells. "Mississippi teach you some things." She throws the door wide open. "Like a colored gal ain't that much when it really come down to it."

Mr. Buster grabs my hand before he picks up my suitcase. Stopping, he slides his fingers deep into his pocket. "For her care." It's a ten-dollar bill.

Jonah walks up the porch steps. "Octobia May. Where you headed to?"

"I have to leave, Jonah."

"Why you got your suitcase?" He turns to Mr. Buster. "I'll take her typewriter. Her and me was planning to write the president on it."

"Boy, get to your room."

"She can't go, Momma."

"Jonah."

Jonah is pulling me by my left hand. Telling his mother he likes having me live with them. Mr. Buster has my other hand, asking Jonah to let me be. It's me who lets Jonah go free. Sending him flying into the house, knocking a hurricane lamp on the floor. It breaks. Mrs. Nicholson yells my name. And threatens to call the police.

"No you won't!" Jonah hollers. "She's my friend!" He runs over to me, hugging me tight. "And we ain't never gonna part."

I look into Jonah's crooked eye. It seems so straight and clear right now. Whispering, he says we have to go to the banker's house. "We planned it, Octobia May."

"Get over here, boy." His mother grabs his right arm, and pulls.

Jonah holds on tight to me, still whispering. If I meet him Friday afternoon, before his father comes home, he will hide me in the back of their station wagon and cover me up with blankets to make sure I get to the banker's house for the big occasion. "Please, Octobia May. You gotta. Or they might kill all the Negroes in town."

Leaving Jonah's place. Taking my time walking down the cold stone steps. I set my lips to whistling. Jonah picks up the tune. His mother slams the door. Jonah runs over to the open window. With ivory curtains blowing into the house, giving him wings, he stands at the window with his lips pushed out. I stand on the pavement puckering, too. We whistle loud and clear. Both at the exact same time. And the grown-ups cannot stop us.

46

HAPPY BIRTHDAY TO ME

Mr. Buster rushes up the alley, carrying my things. I keep my head down, just like him. "Quiet," he told me when we stepped in the first alley. "No talking from here to home so nobody's got a reason to notice you."

Women, hanging clothes on lines in backyards, talk over fences. Or rake up leaves. "Nice fall day. Isn't it?" a white lady putting out trash says to us. I stare at my feet. Mr. Buster steps over a pile of leaves and spits.

Jonah doesn't live far from me. Only today it seems like he lives miles away. We walk through lots of alleys, one park, three lots, and pass by my school. We're on Auntie's block before I notice Mr. Buster's new shiny black shoes. They are exactly the kind Auntie would pick out for him.

"She's home!" he yells, while we are still doors away. "Octobia's here, still in one piece."

I did not know that Miss Marble could run. Or Mrs. Loewenthal's hips worked well enough for her to push people out of the way with them. "Let me look her over." It's Mrs. Ruby, squeezing my fingers and wrists. Working my arms like pulleys. "Did that cop . . . hurt you?"

"No, Mrs. Ruby. He —"

Mrs. Loewenthal holds back tears. "We'll get you out of this, child. My son, the one that is dead to me, is a lawyer. I will have to break my word and . . . phone him."

They are all talking to me at once. Mr. Piers has gotten me a train ticket back home. Mrs. Ruby sticks her change purse in my hand. Whispering in my ear, she tells me that she put four dollars in it. "And once a month when you get to where you are going, I shall send more." Her kisses turn my left cheek red. Mrs. Loewenthal's lips turn my forehead bright pink. The men laugh, saying they are making me look like a circus act. Then they hug and kiss me, too.

Looking up and down the block, Mr. Buster says, "Inside. We have to hide her."

"Hide?" Mrs. Loewenthal says. "I do not like for people to hide."

They have to, they remind her. The police came looking for me this morning. And they'll come back. "But we got a plan." Mr. Buster sits down my things. "Get you to the station tomorrow night; last train. Your aunt Willie will meet you in Chicago. Take you to your grandad's place in Memphis for a while. Then put you on a plane headed for your uncle's place in California." My father will meet me there.

"He knows?" They say I am to phone my parents tonight after the sun goes down. "But I didn't do anything to Officer O'Malley."

Miss Marble takes me by my hand. "What happened, child? Did you take that stake to him?"

"I . . . He . . ." I look at all their faces. If I told them what I had seen, the police might find out and think they had something to do with it. "I passed Officer O'Malley on the street, that's all. I would never hurt anybody."

Mr. Buster kneels down to tie my shoestrings. "You gonna be just fine."

They all start talking to me at once. Mrs. Ruby leaves and comes back into the room. "Now y'all tuck your tears away. Octobia May's home — safe and sound. Let's all eat."

On the back porch, they have a party table set for me. Raisin cookies. My favorite. Boiled eggs. Baked chicken. Hot coffee, cream and sugar. Homemade bread and butter. I pick up a jar of Auntie's jam. "Can't somebody take me to see her?" Twisting the lid, I stick my thumb in and watch it turn blue.

Wiping his hands, Mr. Buster hands me an envelope. Mrs. Loewenthal leaves and comes in carrying a birthday cake with eleven candles in the middle. While they sing to me, I pull out Auntie's letter. I do not know how she did it, but confetti flies to the floor. *Happy birthday to my favorite niece*, it says. *I am free as long as you are.*

47

RIDING TO THE BANKER'S HOUSE

"Jonah. I'm suffocating."

Jonah lifts the blanket. "There. Happy? You always want your way. My momma's coming. So is my father. They find you, they gonna phone the police. I know, Octobia May, 'cause they already done said it."

I am dripping in sweat. My hair is turning, too. "But —"

"I'm in charge. This is our station wagon. And you gonna listen for once."

Jonah's had me laying down in his car since noon. Mr. Buster's been here already twice looking for me. The grown-ups never thought to check here. Jonah's mother said she'd tan his hide if he was keeping me a secret at their house. I heard her myself, when they passed by looking for me behind bushes and inside trash cans. "Now they almost ready. So stay down. Do not breathe. Quit talking."

"Okay, Jonah."

"Okay?"

"Yes. Okay. I will listen to you."

Jonah opens the brown bag in his hand. Out comes a wig, black pants, a white shirt, and boy's shoes. "Keep your head down while you serving. And — limp."

"Limp?"

His mother does not care for children who limp. She lost a boy to polio. He limped before they put him in an iron lung and he died. "A limping boy" — Jonah swallows — "well, she never looks at one full out. Her eyes always go the other way."

I did not know about his brother. My uncle had polio. My neighbor's twin, too. It is not a nice way to live or die.

All the way to the bank president's house, I hold back sneezes. And keep as still as a body in a coffin. Jonah's mother cannot keep my name off of her lips. I am a terrible girl, she says, telling her husband that all Auntie's bad luck began once I moved in.

"That ain't true." Jonah takes up for me. "Octobia

May is my good-luck charm." He asks them to look over his eye. "It's as good as if a doctor healed it."

I can tell that his mother is looking at his eye. "It is back where it should have been from the start," she says. "But that girl's got nothing to do with it. It is just nature correcting itself."

Sweat runs into my eyes. The bumps on the road turn my bones into baseballs bouncing up and down on the floor. But I do not say one word. I am doing exactly what I am told, for once. Until I sneeze.

"Hush."

"What did you say, son?"

"Nothing, Dad. Just a sneeze."

Jonah's parents turn on the radio and sing for most of the trip. He sings along, which is good because I am sneezing again.

"Aah —"

"Chew —"

"Gesundheit." Jonah covers another sneeze with his own. "Turn up the radio, Mom. I like that song. That's Satchmo, ain't it?"

It's Louis "Satchmo" Armstrong, all right. Playing his trumpet and singing. I imagine I am sitting on Mr. Armstrong's knee and drying his sweaty face.

The words of the song about being sorry make me sing to myself.

Jonah's parents join in. They are so loud and happy they do not hear the words Jonah makes up from the Satchmo song. Jonah sings "May bad luck be with you, Mr. Davenport, and your future end right here."

I find my foot tapping, like a sewing machine pedal is beneath it. Jonah pats my head after a while, to quiet me, I think. "That's better."

"What's better, son?"

He talks to his father about the road we are riding on. It winds and dips and is bumpy in places. "The road . . . this spot is smoother."

He turns off the radio . . . For a long while, no one talks. Before I know it I am as calm as a sleeping baby.

Bend River follows you nearly anyplace you go. I smell it, thick in my nose like pickle juice. I hear boats, too. Tied up, bobbing and bumping into the pier, tapping the painted wooden docks like a knock at the door. "Boy, these people sure know how to live." Jonah's mother sighs.

"We live all right, don't we?" Jonah's father makes a sharp left. "You have your own business."

"Yes I do."

"Jonah's got his health."

"He does."

"And you've got me?" They both laugh.

"I do have a fine husband. Not like that Shuma."

Mr. Nicholson says he admires Auntie, although he's never met her in person. "And Octobia May. I think highly of her, too."

Mrs. Nicholson grunts when she says he has always been too freehearted with compliments. She says Aunt Shuma has raised me to reach for higher bushes and better berries, when I need to learn to be content. Her husband asks if she is content with him. She tells him yes. Then he asks if she is content to do hair in their basement for the rest of her life. I learn that she is taking a correspondence course to become a secretary. Soon he will go to trade school to become a plumber. "We all like those higher berries, huh, Sarah Jean?"

When the car stops, Mr. Nicholson reminds them that they all must be very careful. He does not want any of them to end up in the river, where Mr. Harrison's help seems to be landing these days. Mrs. Nicholson agrees. Opening the door, she's back to talking about me. "Much as I hate to say it. The girl's got gumption, all right. Can't take that from her."

48

FISH GIZZARDS AND CHANDELIERS

Jonah's parents walk in through the back door, along with the other help. Looking over his shoulder, my friend keeps an eye on me. I am supposed to stay in the car until the house is filled with people. I won't be noticed as much by his mother then, and Jonah will come for me.

I am in the front seat using Jonah's mother's binoculars — spying when a ruby-red Packard rolls up the long, windy driveway. The tan roof is down, so the lady inside is wearing a net scarf to hold her long curls in place, and a mink stole. Tall and dressed in green, she looks like the Statue of Liberty.

Only Cadillacs pull up next. Black with silver grins and thick whitewall tires. Red with the white roof pulled down. Gray, white, big, long, shiny, and low to the ground in the back, they keep coming like elephants on parade.

Ladies in ball gowns and men in tuxedos with bow ties let the Negro drivers park their cars, and the Negro doormen show them the way inside. It goes on and on, too long, I think. So I turn into a Russian spy. And the binoculars become an X-ray gun — vaporizing people. But I cannot make them disappear, because cars and people keep coming. Out of the station wagon. Squatting on the dirt road, I catch fireflies with my bare hands. Open like the mouth of a cave, my hand lights up. And I wonder if Jonah will ever come back.

Finally Jonah walks onto the back porch, with a coffee can in his hand. Fish gizzards and spines, he tells me when he dumps them. Sniffing his fingers, he warns me about my wig. "It's too big so don't lean over too far when you get inside. Or it may come off."

He turns on the outside faucet and rinses his hands. Then walks with me a little, telling me to smile, do not look the guests in the eye, and keep quiet while I serve.

I straighten my tie and leave my wool jacket outside the door. "Do I really look like a boy, Jonah?"

He levels my new hair. "You'll do. By the way, Mr. Davenport ain't here. Maybe he won't come. But

Mr. Harrison is walking around." Jonah turns into the banker. With his chest poked out. He is holding a pretend cigar between his lips, puffing on it.

Mr. Davenport has to come. Otherwise what good is our plan? I worked it out myself. When the grown-ups aren't looking, I'll go up the steps — the back ones. They have to have them. Then I will find the library, the jewels — the answers to their secrets.

He points to the house. It's time.

Jonah opens the door. I have one foot inside when his elbow hits my rib cage. "A boy in this world don't get no special treatment." Then he walks in first.

With the door open wide, I see how beautiful a house Mr. Harrison lives in. Crystal chandeliers hang in the hallways, with an extra big one in the living room. Men with rifles sit high on horses in one picture. Foxes in the grass jump and run to get away. They are important, these men, with their faces on every wall. They never laugh — like Mr. Buster — I can tell. Or oil anyone's hair like Auntie. They sit stiff and straight. They all wear black. With white collars and cuffs that squeeze, I'd bet. "Jonah."

"Quiet."

I want to ask where he thinks all the ladies went to. Even Mr. Harrison's wife is invisible on the walls here.

Jonah is in charge, so he is doing the explaining.

They have plenty of Negro help to cook in the kitchen, serve food and drinks, and to fuss over guests. We will empty ashtrays, pick up what lands on the floor, and serve cigarettes from silver clamshell cigarette boxes.

"Here." Jonah picks up a cigarette case he set aside just for me. "Be nice. Let people have their fill and more." Next he picks up a water pitcher. "I'm an old hat at this, but no pouring for you."

He points to the staircase. It's spiral, like ours at home. But roomy enough for a Buick to drive up. It's there for everyone to see, so he doesn't know how I will get upstairs to the library. "But if anyone can, you will, Octobia May."

Jonah's mother walks out of the kitchen. Looking left and right, we can tell she is looking for him. With his back as strong as a rod, he walks toward the kitchen like a fine gentleman. Leaving me on my own.

49

THE FUR COAT AND THE BANKER'S WIFE

"My, my. Now where have you come from?" I steady the tray in my hands and limp along. "Who do you belong to?" It's Mrs. Harrison, arranging the cigarettes on my clamshell. Pall Malls. Camels. Lucky Stripes. Sit side by side. "I did request more help. But another child? How is it that I am just noticing you?" She takes a cigarette. A man with a nice smile flicks his lighter and her cigarette is lit.

"Do you have a name?" she says to me.

Jonah and I didn't think about my voice. Anyone could tell I am a girl. Like Bessie, I stare ahead.

Mrs. Harrison's hand is on my arm, warm and soft when she holds me, and calls for a man named Joseph. She supposes I am a good worker, she tells him when he walks over. But if I don't talk, perhaps a better place for me is in the kitchen, she lets him know.

"Yes, ma'am. I'll get him back there right away, ma'am."

She reminds him that her guests will need more ice. And that Mrs. Potter's blue mink fur coat simply "cannot" be hung with all the rest. "It's an heirloom. Take it upstairs to my cedar closet. And lock it up." She talks about a missing ring. Is it the one with the girl on it? I want to ask. She's just noticed it's missing, along with other jewels, she whispers. Quietly I hear her say, "Why my husband will not phone in the police, I don't know, Joseph."

When the front door swings opens, Mrs. Harrison gets very excited. "Oh, it's Hardy Davenport. A war hero. Remember, everyone, we're raising money for a good cause. So all Americans will be free and equal — both the Negroes and women. Times are changing and we want to do our part."

Her arm loops through Mr. Davenport's like thread through a needle. She sounds like my parents when she talks about the good work the NAACP is doing and why they will also get a share of the money raised. I think about Mr. Thurgood Marshall and the girl at that school. Will the banker and his wife help them, too?

Mrs. Harrison's words stop the party. People listen to her instead of drinking or eating their food. She talks about her family on her mother's side. They were abolitionists, Quakers.

"What's that?" I ask Joseph.

"What?"

"Quakers. Abo . . . lishes."

He grumbles at first, asking how come I don't already know. Then he explains that they are people who helped the slaves.

Mrs. Harrison takes her husband by the arm. She says while he was at war, she wrote letters to the president and to General Benjamin O. Davis, pushing them to end segregation in the military. "I joined the NAACP. Along with A. Philip Randolph, they worked hard to get the government to put some muscle behind Executive Order 8802, ending discrimination in employment in the defense industry and elsewhere," she says. "To get Negroes jobs at plants, shipyards. Building planes for the war, operating streetcars and buses." Even now, she says, they are fighting for better opportunities and jobs.

Looking at her husband, with stars in her eyes, she says she is proud to announce that he is the first banker in the city to hire a Negro teller. Just yesterday he hired a Negro accountant. "The first in the state."

Everyone in the room claps. I do not understand. Mr. Harrison works hard for Negroes. How can he kill them?

When they are done talking, Joseph's eyes stick me. "Sit that thing down, boy. Over there. And take this upstairs." He looks up at Mrs. Harrison and sucks his teeth. "Always wanting something. Go here. Run there. How I'm supposed to take up the fur, tote the books to the boathouse, serve — NAACP my eye."

I can barely carry the fur. Or breathe from the thick smoke. But I am happy because I can walk up the stairs and no one will stop me. Setting one foot on the stair, I see Jonah running toward me. "Hurry. She knows. And she's coming."

It's his mother. Carrying a trayful of food. Stopping along the way to offer some to all the hands reaching out for it. She looks at me.

I am careful and quick getting upstairs. Laying the fur across a couch in the hall, I walk over to a door. With my eyes closed, I turn the knob. Hoping no one is inside.

50

HIDING IN THE LIBRARY

I pull the wig off. And open more doors. There are so many rooms. A study with the fireplace burning. Another music room with another grand piano. Bathrooms with gold swan faucets spitting water when I turn them on. A sewing room filled with beautiful fabrics. Finally, the library.

Brown, shiny bookcases go all the way up to the ceiling and take up almost every wall. Except one. Walking around the room with my fingertips brushing the books, I look over the shelves. Law books, banking books, storybooks, insurance books, even a book about how to dig a well. And the Bible — sitting next to a book by a man named Hawthorne.

I cross the room, noticing that the people in the paintings keep their eyes on me. Especially the Negro woman standing in a painting all alone. She could be my granny, with her dark skin and pearls. I think maybe she worked here once.

It's the vault that I'm trying to get to. I figure all the banker's secrets must be stashed in there. Almost as wide and tall as the back wall, it's easy to find. The lock is as wide as one of Auntie's cabbages. Turning and twisting it, I listen while it clicks. "If only I knew the combination." Looking up I see something else turning — the knob to the door.

I am behind the couch, on my hands and knees, when the men rush in. They talk about the money in the vault, while Mr. Harrison turns the knob this way and that until the vault is open. Using a key, Mr. Harrison opens one of the drawers. There are lots of them. Too many for me to count.

He gives Mr. Davenport a stack of money, then three more. Before he locks the drawer, Mr. Davenport pulls out jewels. Then something from his pocket. The ring.

It's the ring I took.

"Great," Mr. Harrison says. "My wife keeps asking me about it. It took all I could to prevent her from filing a report with the insurance company and calling the police." The banker stands on a stool to open a drawer high above his head and puts the things away.

Mr. Davenport asks about the envelope. "It's locked away," the banker says. He thanks him and promises not to let it get away from him ever again.

Sitting down, they go over their scheme. After dessert. Before cordials. They will come back upstairs to count the donation money. That's when Mr. Harrison will report that his own money is missing.

"You know they will blame the kitchen help and servers."

Mr. Harrison has it figured out. As soon as Mr. Davenport is safe and sound he will tell the police that he is the "real culprit. As well as the murderer."

Mr. Davenport is sliding money in all four of his inside breast pockets when he says, "Fine. I'm headed back to Europe — Belgium, Germany. And — I promised myself I'd never return. But I have to." He takes a deep breath. "Now, what about O'Malley?"

"He should be dead."

"Well, he isn't. And I am finished killing."

I almost can't breathe when I find out that Officer O'Malley is at the boathouse tied up — alive, I learn.

After Mr. Davenport drives away in the banker's boat tonight, he is supposed to dump Officer O'Malley in the river by the viaduct. Now he wants that to be the banker's job. "Get your hands a little dirty. Finally."

Mr. Harrison mentions a lieutenant. Mr. Davenport does not want to talk about him. I think they killed him, too. But I don't know when, or where, or why, because they quickly move to talk about something else.

Mr. Davenport looks at his own hands. Turning them over and over again, he goes back to the war. "To put an end to Hitler and his reign, Uncle Sam asked soldiers to do things some could hardly live with. Like looking into a man's eyes while you launch a grenade at him. Raining bombs from the skies onto neighborhoods and towns." Mr. Davenport buttons his tuxedo jacket. "Starve for your country in a German prison camp."

The banker rubs his chin. And walks back and forth in front of the vault. Mr. Harrison seems kind while he pats Mr. Davenport's shoulder. "That was hell for you, I know. No wonder you still have difficulty sleeping at night."

"I walk until just before dawn. A vampire. That's what she said I was." He smiles. "Maybe I am. Was." He says in the last weeks it has gotten better. "Funny. Knowing I am going back over there is resting my mind."

He is going back to find soldiers — American and her allies — to put flags on their graves. He wants to find a little girl, too. Her father was in a POW camp with him. If he didn't make it out alive, he promised to go check on her. He never did. "When you walked out of one of Hitler's camps you felt lucky to be alive.

"Jim Crow was still alive and well in America, the military, too. I knew that. But I was still happy to be heading home."

The banker nods. He prayed day and night for him while he was away. "We all did."

Mr. Davenport walks over to one of the pictures on the wall. It's the Negro woman in the painting. Mr. Harrison stands by his side. "She would not be proud of us."

"I've done a lot of good." Negro soldiers knew they could come to him during the war even though they thought he was white, he says. "I intervened on their behalf with the other officers — Negro and white. I've saved lives . . . careers many times, too."

Four times a year he leaves town, I learn. Traveling south. "To teach other Negroes to read, so they can vote and get the jobs that are finally opening up to them." The women he's hired at his bank come from below the Mason-Dixon Line, he says. "Killing them to keep my secret was worth it, I think."

Mr. Davenport says that maybe bad can cancel out all the good you do. The way too much salt can ruin a cake. "I'm tired," he says, "of fighting wars." Then he says maybe he should hold on to the envelope. He thinks if someone finds it now their lives are over.

The banker's wife walks in. Kissing her. Leaving the vault open. They all head for the door. "Is that wise?" she asks, looking over her shoulder.

They know everyone at the party. Even the help has all worked with them before, he tells her. "So let's go dine and enjoy our guests."

51

THE SECRET OF THE LADY IN THE PICTURE

The library door swings open hard and wide. "Octobia May. Where are you? Please. Get out this house, 'fore the coloreds and the whites both have your head."

I run across the room, letting Jonah know that Mr. Davenport really was a hero. And Officer O'Malley is alive. But before we can get him, we need to find the envelope that the banker is protecting and Mr. Davenport thinks could put an end to the two of them. "It's the final secret to the puzzle, I bet."

Jonah pulls me toward the door. "That secret may

get us killed, too, Octobia May. Please. Let's leave. My mother will come looking for you soon."

I am talking a mile a minute, unable to stop myself. I tell him about the little girl on the ring — I guess she wasn't magic after all — and the one overseas that Mr. Davenport will try to find. The flags in our graveyard. Now we know for sure he put them there, and why Mr. Davenport walked the night like a vampire.

Jonah follows while I search the vault, Mr. Davenport's desk drawers, and the ledge of his bookshelves. But we do not find any spare keys.

Looking through gold-edged books, we hurry. And sit them on the floor instead of placing them back. Mr. Harrison has every book in the world, it seems. We'll never find the keys this way, I admit to Jonah. "And what if every lock has a different key? Then we wouldn't be looking for one key, but as many keys as there are fish in Bend River."

I am roaming around the room, with questions in my head. Where would you keep a group of keys you did not want people to find? Or hide papers so important people die because of them? Standing by a ladder that has wheels, I look up. "A secret place to keep the keys to all your secrets. That's what I'm looking for."

Tapping walls. I check for secret passages. Pulling at the woodwork. Jonah tries his best to help me. Finally

he holds on to a ladder we find, while I walk up.
Checking more books. Looking at pictures, I am hoping not to fall. Just like the banker and Mr. Davenport,
I look at the woman in the picture across the room. She
doesn't fit. All the other pictures in the room are of Mr.
Harrison and his wife. Or horses eating grass or racing
up green hills.

Stepping down from the ladder I walk over to her.
Apologizing for the Harrisons, I wipe and blow dust off
her frame. Carefully I lift the picture off the wall. It's
not as heavy as it looks. And tell Jonah what I am thinking. Turning the picture over, I see that I was right.
"Look." All along the edges are keys. Taped together as
close as teeth.

I hold my breath, when I turn the thirteenth key. "It
works." But before I can open the box, the library door
flies open.

"Jonah Nicholson. If you in here —" His mother
walks into the library and stops. "What a mess." She
says she didn't realize the Harrisons were so disorderly.
She gets back to talking about Jonah, who's in the vault
along with me. "I'm calling the police on that Octobia
May. I have to. They good white folks living here. Why
those two want to ruin things for us?"

She is talking to herself. Ignoring the vault. Not seeing us hiding inside. When she leaves she closes the door
quietly. Jonah locks it behind her. I hold my breath once

more, and finally open the box. "Oh, Jonah. Did you ever see so much loot?"

He lifts the stack of money with both hands. He's fingering it like cards in a deck. "One thousand. Two thousand. Ten." It's too much money to count.

"Not now, Jonah. We're looking for a different secret."

We try more boxes. Our good luck is with us. Some open, others don't. Jonah sits down a handful of jewelry and fastens a diamond necklace around my neck.

"It's so heavy." I hold on to the emerald-green stone.

Blue diamond earrings. A clear pink ring the size of my nose. Freshwater pearl necklaces. They all sit in sacks and velvet boxes that we open. I think about the banker's conversation. His wife comes from a rich family with a long history in banking. "But they do not trust banks much themselves. So they pile fortunes in their homes like beavers store up food for the winter," he said. "She never checks her treasures. Until recently, when she inquired about the ring," he went on to say. "Then she found other things missing."

We get back to our searching. Finding more questions than answers, that's for sure.

Jonah unlocks the next box. But there are only baby things inside. A white blanket, knitted with blue lace at the edges. A bonnet. A wooden rattle.

I stand on a table to get to the drawers up high. Only

none of the keys work for a very long time. Until we get lucky again. "What are stocks?" I ask Jonah. He does not know. "RCA, Chicago Railroad System, Bell Telephone."

"Octobia May. We do not got time to read. Hurry. My mother said the party ends at ten and that's coming sooner than you'd think."

Another box. More baby things. *Time for us to leave,* I think. Booties. A tiny silver baby bracelet with the name Alberta engraved on it. Jumping down. Picking up the blanket again, I rub my cheeks with it. Because I know what happened. I see now, their baby died. "It's a sad thing," I tell Jonah, stretching out the blanket to see how big the baby was when she passed. An envelope curled in the corners, falls on the floor. Inside is a yellow piece of paper split down the middle. I take my time unfolding it. "A . . . birth certificate?" Standing up, trying hard to keep myself from fainting, I hand it to Jonah.

"It ain't a dead baby's certificate, either, Octobia May. Or a junior, named after her."

"No . . . it's not."

"It's his. Mr. Harrison's."

We hold on to it together. "And it says here he's . . . he's . . . he's . . ."

"Colored," we say together.

Scratching his head, Jonah stays quiet a long while.

"Do you think some of those other white people downstairs are passing, too?"

"I do not know, Jonah."

He sits the birth certificate down. "Why would you want to be something you wasn't, Octobia May?" Before I can answer, he starts up again. "And his wife. What about her? Seems if you married to a Negro you might want to know about it first."

This is not the secret we were looking for. It's so big. I do not know what to do with it.

It's Jonah's mother's voice that gets us moving. She is up the hall again, along with someone else. Jonah's father, or Joseph, maybe. Sliding the birth certificate in my pocket, I dash across the room holding Jonah's hand.

Leaving the library through a door that leads to another room, we head for the window. I tell Jonah about the lieutenant who may have been killed. He brings up the white teller who disappeared.

Jonah forgets I am a boy tonight and lets me jump from the window first. Walking in the grass while Jonah's shoe play taps on the sidewalk, I ask what we should do. He will go to the house and keep them off my trail. I will go to the boathouse and rescue Officer O'Malley.

Stopping, I pull the picture out of my pocket. The cut over his eyebrow. Why didn't I notice it from the start? The same eyes but older. With the shine missing.

Jonah's hug is very likely to break me in two. "Octobia May. Don't you get yourself drowned, or cut up into tiny pieces fit for fish bait."

Backing away, I look up at the moon. It's not crescent, but it will do. "We can't die, Jonah. We're brave. The luckiest kids who ever were born."

Running downhill, my shoes get soaked from the river water creeping along the grass by the boathouse. I stay put a long while, listening to cars pull up to the front house and laughing guests making their way outside.

"Octobia May, you got more rights than all the Negroes in this city put together," I can hear Jonah's mother say in my head.

Of course that isn't true. But I am free. Able to think for myself. To choose to do, or not do — as brave and strong as Auntie always wanted me to be.

52

ON A BOAT TO NOWHERE

Heavy ropes and rusted anchors sit on the boathouse floor. Life jackets and lanterns hang on heavy hooks, swinging when I close the door. Spiders. Worms in dirt jars. It's all here, and more. But not Officer O'Malley. I look and look for him, even inside the wooden bench cluttered with more things. But they put him somewhere else. And I know where. Outside. Staring toward the boat. I start walking.

"Woo. Steady girl." I walk the plank and then go onboard. Standing on deck, I look across Bend River. Black with moonlight sitting on it, it looks long and sad.

Walking around the deck. Passing a chair and life jackets, I make my way upstairs. Sitting at the captain's chair, working the steering wheel, I look at all the lights across the river. But I need to find a good place to disappear. So it's not long before I'm heading down below.

I sit on the bed, bouncing at first. Next I'm in the bathroom, turning on the faucet at the bathroom sink. Opening a door, I step into the closet. It's small, but it will make a good place to hide. But what if I lock myself in? I try to slide underneath the bed next. I fit. But it's not just me here. There are fishing rods and a tackle box. Life jackets and old shoes. I come out from underneath the bed and wait some time. Until I hear footsteps. Then my eyes jump from the closet to the bed, to the closet again. Diving under the bed, I bump my head hard. "Ouch! Oooh."

"Octobia May? Come out!"

It's Jonah. He tells me how he got away from his parents. His father was very tired. He couldn't drive one more block. So while his dad and his mom were asleep by the side of the road, he came back to me. "Mr. Davenport will be here soon," he tells me. He heard the two men talking outside behind the house.

I give him a choice. He can have the closet or hide under the bed. He might have to capture them as soon as they get onboard, he says, so I should leave the bed for him. Like pajamas and dress shoes, I get put in the closet.

"Here." I hand Jonah his Satchel Paige baseball card. "For luck."

"Thanks. I been missing him." Using a matchbook to keep the latch from locking, he encourages me to be brave.

I talk to him from the vent in the door. "Where are you, Jonah?"

"Under the bed."

"I think I hear —"

"Quiet, Octobia May. They coming. Now don't be scared. Okay?"

"I was dead before, remember, Jonah?"

Jonah does not answer me. He is doing like I'm doing, I guess, trying not to be discovered.

"Hold him, Albert. He's strong still. O'Malley. Do not give us one more moment's trouble, or I may pitch you overboard right now."

It's Mr. Davenport. Out of breath, he warns Officer O'Malley again. "So you want to fight. Even with your arms tied." I hear a punch. Someone stumbles and trips down the stairs.

Mr. Davenport calls to Mr. Harrison, asking if he can handle things upstairs for a minute. "Every second counts."

Officer O'Malley's arms are tied. When the boat starts, it jerks forward, knocking my head against the door. The chill from the night air fills up the cabin after a while. The rock of the boat. The twists and turns. Sends food into my throat. Swallowing. Frowning. Holding my mouth, I wonder if more is on the way.

It's Officer O'Malley who loses his supper, just when Mr. Davenport pulls the sock out of his mouth.

"A cop who can't keep his food down!" He hits him. "Do you understand how much I pay for my things?" He pushes Officer O'Malley facedown onto the bed, and stands, wiping his shoes. "Italian. Made by hand. Ruined." He bangs his fist on the closet door. "I think you threw up on me intentionally." Mr. Davenport stuffs the rag in his mouth again.

The boat engine slows down and then speeds up again. Officer O'Malley curls up on the bed. Mr. Davenport never takes his eyes off him, even while he soaps his hands. And wipes off his shoes again. Double-checking the ropes around Officer O'Malley's hands, he calms down and talks to him like it is any ordinary day. Does he have any children? he asks. Did he grow up always wanting to be an officer of the law? "Oh." He laughs. "Let's take that out."

Officer O'Malley coughs and rolls until he's sitting up. "I should have believed the child. She knew a murdering scoundrel when she saw one."

Lifting up and out of the water. Dropping down again. The boat cuts through Bend River, smacking the water over and over, more times than I can count. Mr.

Davenport stops talking. After a long while I can hear a train whistle blow. The wheels clicking on the track comfort me some. Because I think I know where we are. Near Fifth and Canary, the train rides the river close, as the vegetable wagons and streetcars do.

Holding on to a clothes rack, I steady myself. Pinching my nose so I can keep the smell out. It's sulfur. From the steel mill outside of town. We must be passing it. Leaving the city now. I look at Officer O'Malley. Sitting on the bed. Nursing a black eye. Tied up. Only Jonah and I can help him now.

53

THE BOY WHO RAN
AWAY ON THE TRAIN

I am still on Mr. Davenport's mind, I suppose. He offers Officer O'Malley a cigarette and speaks my name. "The first time I heard Octobia May mention vampires, I knew I could trick her." I was outside his room, he says. Crying.

I remember the night. It was raining and we had just come back from another monster night drive-in movie. I didn't want to sleep in my bed. Auntie was insisting. She said she knew I would have nightmares. "With your imagination you'll have vampires living here with us before long." I think she forgot she said that.

Mr. Davenport isn't smoking. Just holding the cigarette and letting it burn out. "They were standing in the hall across from my room. It was perfect, really. The storm. Thunder. The pest. She was always determined to figure me out — even before then. She'd set clean towels outside my door and wait for me to come out. Or bring up toast and jam — with a note, of course. Volunteering to dust or shine my closet doorknobs." He wonders what I saw in him from the beginning.

Nancy Drew. Radio mysteries. You read and hear enough of those and you know when trouble is at your door.

Officer O'Malley repeats what Mr. Buster said. Children have a second sense. "Especially when it comes to murderous thugs and crooks." Then he spits. Yellow and thick, it flies and hits the wrong spot: Mr. Davenport's silk tie. He rolls onto his side, to get away from Mr. Davenport's fist, and bangs his head when he falls on the floor like a sack of potatoes being tossed onboard. "You nig —"

Mr. Davenport's fist keeps the rest of the word down in his throat. But Officer O'Malley keeps talking. "How'd the devil did ya get a white man to go along with your schemes?"

The boat slows and stops. From the main deck, the banker yells downstairs. It's all in Mr. Davenport's hands, he says. But Mr. Davenport is "just along for the ride this time," he tells him.

From the top of the stairs, the banker's voice gets louder. "Bring him up and do what you are being paid to do!"

Mr. Davenport loves his shoes, more than anything, I think. He is back to polishing them with a clean handkerchief. Lighting two cigarettes, he hands one to Officer O'Malley and they both puff. Looking toward the steps, he starts talking. And does not quit even when the banker runs down demanding that he does so.

"We would see Albert on the street. My mother and I. She would say, there's your cousin. Shhh. Don't wave. Or speak. And never ever tell anyone. Of course he's colored like you and I. But better off. Far better off." Then something happened. Mr. Harrison's mother died. And he was sent to live with their granny.

Officer O'Malley's eyes go from one man to the other, settling on Mr. Davenport. Mr. Harrison turns away. Mr. Davenport keeps talking. "As if Gypsies put a curse on him, overnight he turned Negro. Until —"

I think about the train ride. Mr. Harrison holds on to the sink and looks at himself in the mirror. It was his idea to run away to the big city. "Chicago." They had light-skinned family there.

Grabbing Officer O'Malley by the arm, Mr. Harrison starts talking, too. "But then, fate. Kismet stepped in and I sat myself down at its table and feasted. And lived the life I was meant to live all along." He is red-faced and trembling, raising his voice. He asks if he knows what it is like for a Negro, especially in the South. "Yes, sir. No, sir. Sorry, sir. Meant to keep my eyes on the ground, sir." He is somebody else now, bowing and looking put upon. "No, sir, sure don't mind going to that shack of a school over yonder, sir, while yours gets the nice books and clean floors and to swim in the cool, clear pools. No, sir. I do not mind one bit if I cannot try shoes or hats on in the store like the whites!" His fist goes to his mouth, like he is trying to stop his own words from telling on him. "But I did."

Mr. Davenport's eyes find his shoes. His hand goes on Mr. Harrison's shoulder, patting it. They are family, he says. The banker looked out for him when he was in the service. "How many times was I AWOL? In town breaking rules that should never have been. But it's all in the past. This is a new day. Let's take him upstairs. What's one more body in Bend River, huh, cousin?"

Officer O'Malley asks to hear the whole "blasted story." Shoving him, the banker says he might as well hear the truth before he dies. "It's simple." The maid was dusting the library shelves. Mr. Harrison had left to take a phone call before she came in. The vault was open, and the birth certificate was sitting out. She took it to her husband, the chef. Who blackmailed the banker for months before Mr. Davenport was called into town.

"I am a patient man," Mr. Davenport says. "I strike when I want to, not upon request."

"Some things I could do alone," the banker says. He mentions a teller. Then bringing up the lieutenant he says the two men brought it on themselves.

The boat rocks hard, like maybe Bend River is trying to shake things up in here. Jonah moans. And then throws up. Mr. Davenport runs over to the bed, calling my name. "Octobia May, I see you." He bends down, pulling a leg. "What? You. Where is she?"

He will toss Jonah to the sharks if he doesn't give me away, he says.

I do not budge.

Spittle hangs from Jonah's lips when he comes from under the bed. "She ain't come." He stands and pushes his chest out. "She missed the boat. Dang her." He pretends to cry. "I'm gonna die tonight because of her."

Mr. Davenport looks around the room. Opening the closet door, he shuts it and never looks inside. That's because Jonah is distracting him. Giving him a good, hard kick in the shins.

Slamming the closet door, Mr. Davenport grabs him by his shirt collar. And then holds him in the air so his feet barely reach the floor. Officer O'Malley grumbles, asking Jonah why he didn't have the good sense to steer clear of "the likes of him." Mr. Davenport is asking the banker to help with the two of them when Officer O'Malley leans over and headbutts him. That's when Jonah tries to make a getaway.

All of a sudden, I see it. A pistol. Mr. Davenport pulls it out. Forcing them to shut up and go upstairs. After a while, I am alone, below, by myself. Finally I go upstairs to save my friend.

54

THE END OF US?

Ropes are twisted around Jonah's hands. Water from Bend River has made its way on deck, wetting his pants and shoes. "Did she die, Mr. Harrison?" Jonah doesn't move while his ankles get roped together. He talks about his brother, dying from polio four years ago. Mr. Davenport warns him to shut up. "It's bad to be in an iron lung," Jonah says. "Like living in a casket."

I keep my eyes on the pistol. He sat it down to tie the ropes, then picked it up. Aiming it at Jonah.

"Somebody kill your girl? Polio take her? Or ain't she make it out the hospital alive like some babies do?"

Mr. Davenport throws the gun to the banker. "Together, cousin. I've done enough killing on my own."

Mr. Harrison holds the gun over Officer O'Malley. With the water licking the boat, he talks about his baby girl. She never made it out of her mother's belly. "My secret stayed safe." He shakes and has to hold the gun with both hands.

Mr. Davenport spits on the deck. Weak men like the banker make monsters out of other men, he says, pulling Jonah over to the edge.

Officer O'Malley looks up at the banker, then at Mr. Davenport. "Bloody day in the morning, man. Let the boy go home."

The banker is talking about himself. Saying he can never go home again. "My family hates what I've become. As light as they are, they are proud to be Negroes scrapping and scrimping by."

Jonah asks if he hates being a Negro. Mr. Harrison says Jonah is too young to understand. He paces the deck. "I just . . . wanted all I could have in this life. And I could not have it if—" He liked sitting in the front of the train. Dining at tables with linen cloths with waiters that called him sir. "Having white people smile and extend their hands to me on the train. It was like old times again."

Officer O'Malley asks him to be quiet. "It's disgusting, the whole bloody tale." He spits. "We Irish. Have our own sad stories to tell. So do the Polish and the

Jews." He turns and bends his neck. "America . . . sometimes she is a bother to us all."

Coming out of the shadows. Holding a stick high over my head. I slip on the wet deck — falling. Mr. Davenport sees me first and runs after me, tilting when the boat does. Slipping. Sliding on river water. He tries to protect his shoes. So I get my chance to make another getaway.

Shoving the gun across the deck, Mr. Harrison tells Mr. Davenport to grab it. But then Bend River burps. Lifting the boat up on one side like a friend lending me a hand, it sends the gun in the opposite direction. I jump over an empty crate. Almost trip over the rope that holds the anchor in the water.

"Octobia May!" Jonah warns me to watch out. Mr. Harrison is close behind.

Officer O'Malley says I am their only hope. "Grab it, girl. Shoot if you must."

On my hands and knees, I reach for the gun. Standing, I fling it far into the choppy water. Another secret for Bend River to keep.

Stuffing a sock into Officer O'Malley's mouth, the banker asks what they are to do now. Jonah wrestles with his ropes. Mr. Davenport opens a tackle box and pulls out a knife. The kind you gut fish with. Wide. It shines in the moonlight. "How could it end any other way, cousin?" he says.

Mr. Harrison agrees. It's not long before they both capture me.

55

THE NOT-SO-GREAT ESCAPE

Mr. Davenport is a vampire again, looking at each of us like he could drink our blood. "Who's first?"

"Me."

Jonah interrupts, asking why everything has to go my way. Wrestling with his ropes he says he should be the next to go. "I'm the boy. Girls ain't supposed to be in charge of everything, Octobia May. I'll do the dying first." With his crooked eye, the one people sometimes do not pay attention to, he winks at me.

The banker unties Jonah's hands. Jonah looks out on the water, asking Mr. Davenport how long it would take for a body to go under.

"It's not fair." I bite at the ties on my hands and wink at Jonah.

"Quiet, girl." The banker shoves Officer O'Malley when he tries to make a ruckus.

"You picked him first because he's a boy. Auntie says —"

"See what I've had to contend with?" Mr. Davenport begins to untie me. He says I am the bother he always knew me to be. So the sooner they are rid of me, the better.

After untying Jonah's feet, they walk us over to the side of the boat like pirates about to dump their loot. "This is it," I say. "I am on my way to meet Juppie."

Jonah says cats have their own heaven. People go someplace else. "Don't they, Mr. Davenport?"

Mr. Davenport is looking at his shoes. Water spots are on the toes, he says. Mr. Harrison wonders why he is wiping them when "any minute now we could be found out."

I look up at the night sky. "I was dead once. Did you know that, Mr. Harrison?"

His blue-gray eyes look black in the night. "No." He holds on to my elbow and takes more steps. Then surprises me when he unties my hands.

"I held Juppie when she died. I hope you got to hold your baby. Did you get to hold your baby?"

He looks at Mr. Davenport, who is stuffing his handkerchief in his pocket. "I didn't know how bad it was for you there," he says to him. Then he answers me. She died before birth. Punishment, he sometimes thinks. "For all I'd done not to be discovered." Then he says, "See, Hardy? We had to keep doing what we did. Otherwise, she died for nothing."

Mr. Davenport argues with him. He should go to church if he needs a confessional, he says. Then the banker blames it all on me. Everything would have been fine, he thinks, had Mr. Davenport not pulled me into their situation. If he had gotten all of his money right off, Mr. Davenport says, instead of jewels that could only have ended him in jail — he would have left the country weeks ago.

Officer O'Malley falls over. Like he's fainted. Mr. Harrison rushes up to him. "Sit up. Or you'll go first!" Officer O'Malley is like a soggy log, nothing the banker does sets him upright. "Hardy. Come help me." He pulls the sock out of Officer O'Malley's mouth.

I look at Jonah and do what I did when I was home with my mother. Force my fingers down my throat. Up comes breakfast. All over Mr. Davenport's fancy black, spit-shined, expensive Italian shoes.

He drops the knife. Mr. Harrison explodes. I am backing up step by step, when Jonah jumps into the river. "Run, Octobia May. They can't catch both of us."

Officer O'Malley trips Mr. Harrison when he bolts

after me. Mr. Davenport ignores his shoes and starts running, too. I throw Jonah a life jacket.

"Octobia May!" Jonah swims toward the jacket. "Get to the radio. Call the police."

I run up the stairs, with Mr. Davenport behind me. Closing. Locking the door. Reaching for the radio, I watch his fist break the glass.

What do I do? I think. His fingers fool with the lock. Beating them away with a logbook, I jump into the captain's chair.

"Girl, don't you —"

And turn the key in the ignition.

"Nooo —"

I press my foot on the gas and the boat flies — fast and hard enough to knock Mr. Davenport down. I turn the steering wheel, and the boat leans and settles itself. When Mr. Davenport gets to his feet, I speed across the water. And down he goes again.

I cannot hold on to the wheel. Falling off the seat, I join him on the floor. And watch the boat find its own way over the river. Turning into an airplane, it flies. "Trees."

Wind whistles loudly pass my ears. I cover my eyes, while things not tied down sail pass me. I'm not sure why he does it, but Mr. Davenport leans over and covers me. Telling me that this is not a day that either one of us will die.

56

FREEING AUNTIE

Aunt Shuma walks out of the jailhouse. Staring up at the sun, she smiles. "Octobia May." Bending down, she gives me a mighty big hug. "You did it." Jonah runs up to Auntie, reminding her he did his part, too. "I know. You both did. Rescued me." She keeps walking with our hands in hers, with Mr. Buster carrying a small bag of her things.

They are at the curb, some of them anyhow. Mrs. Ruby, Mrs. Loewenthal, Mr. Piers, too. Mr. Buster told them they might want to stay at home. He planned a party for Auntie, with the Do Some Good Ladies Club members and other people that we know. But our boarders would not stay put.

Auntie stops before she gets into the car. Looking up and down the street, she lets both of our hands go. "I knew," she says, "that your mother was wrong keeping you still at home. The world is a mighty big place. And we got to feel mighty big inside to take it on."

Our car is a hearse. Perfect for us today, with all the people Mr. Buster needs to cart around. Before Auntie steps inside, she leans in close to him. Kissing his cheek, she compliments his shoes. "Black, sturdy, and shiny. Day by day, Buster, you are making your way, I see."

In front of me and everyone else, Mr. Buster gives her a big, giant kiss on the lips.

"Shuma. Shuma, wait."

Jonah puffs up when his mother crosses the street. "Morning, Octobia May. Buster. Jonah." She shakes her head and smiles. She just wanted to say hello to Auntie, she tells her, and to apologize for things. "This girl of yours. She saved Jonah."

"We saved each other," I tell her.

"You helped, Mom. When I ain't come home, you sent them police. And told 'em all you knew." His crooked eye is back to being its new self. "And you wasn't scared of the white people neither, or what they thought of Negroes."

Auntie invites her to her party. Jonah's mother says to come by tomorrow and she will wash, press, and curl Auntie's hair at no cost. Mine, too.

Sitting on Auntie's lap. With the window down and the fall day blowing cool in the car, we all make our way home. Quiet and noisy. Happy and sad. With Mrs. Loewenthal asking me about coffee, gefilte fish, and that night on the boat. Mr. Buster is polite when he interrupts to talk to me. "Octobia May, in case Mr. Davenport made you think otherwise — the Negro soldier been a credit to the nation. Take, for example, them men on the Red Ball Express."

Auntie insists. "No history lessons, Buster. It's my day, and I want it free and easy."

Mr. Buster breaks her rule. "Late in the war," he said. "In order to fight. Negro sergeants had to give up their stripes to make sure they would not command any white solders."

Auntie sighs. I hug her. But in no time at all, that night passes through my mind again. The boat landing in a patch of trees right where the forest starts. I had only a few scratches. But Jonah was still in the cold water. And Officer O'Malley was tied up and passed out, with a gash on his head from being thrown out of the boat. I never would have figured it. Mr. Davenport went to get Jonah. The banker sat at the water's edge. Holding his head, wondering how he would ever explain things to his wife.

"I said I was done with killing. I guess I am. Saving my enemies. What am I thinking?" Mr. Davenport laid Jonah down beside me and pushed on his chest. After a while Jonah was asleep, his head resting in my lap.

We could see the lights from a boat far off. Mr. Davenport said it was most likely the Coast Guard. His cousin moaned.

"Maybe . . . you will write a book about us one day." Mr. Davenport picked up his muddy shoes from the ground. He always wanted to write an adventure story but never seemed to have the time, he said.

I asked what he was doing in his room all that time, even though I knew. Trying to write about the war, he said. Thinking if he put it all down on paper, he would finally get some rest.

"Why'd you burn your book?"

He asks if there wasn't one of his secrets that I didn't know. I mention the Negro lady in the picture at the banker's house. I figured he knew her, too. He nodded, and said he finished the book, but had no peace. In the end, he says he felt he'd dishonored the Negro soldier — in more ways than one. Especially the 333rd. A Negro Field Artillery Battalion, he told me. Men he had served with during the war. Some of them imprisoned, too; some who had escaped — "eleven men butchered by Hitler's SS."

His words made my bones cold. I held on tighter to

Jonah. But I was still full of questions. I wanted to know why he had killed the lieutenant.

We could see the boat more clearly. So he spoke quickly. A lieutenant overheard a conversation between him and his cousin. He found out Mr. Harrison wasn't white. "It was an argument, really." Their grandmother — "the woman in the painting" — was dying and Mr. Davenport was headed home the next day on leave. Mr. Harrison had decided not to go. His career. His new wife. His new life. He didn't want anything to ruin it. It was a big war, he said. Soldiers — colored and white — were everywhere in this country on leave, or serving, or about to be shipped overseas. He couldn't risk going south and being found out.

"I was a Negro in charge of white men — thousands. In the States and later, overseas. God knows what they would have done had they found out about that." He lowered his voice when he mentioned the lieutenant's name. "The army teaches you a lot of things to get a job done," Mr. Harrison said, standing. "To use a bayonet. Your hands. Whatever is necessary."

"And family," Mr. Davenport whispered, "is family. Though you may live to regret that they are one day."

"Bloody day in the morning." Officer O'Malley finally woke up. "If I could get up — I'd arrest you, Davenport." Moaning, he closed his eyes.

I had more questions. But the Coast Guard boat was stopping. Mr. Davenport took a stick and knocked mud off his shoes. Then he looked up. "Cousin. It's over. Here they are."

Men were rushing over to meet us. "Arrest them!" Officer O'Malley had a hard time standing up, but he did. "They tried to kill these children."

57

OFFICER O'MALLEY AND THE SCREAMING GIRL

"Octobia May. Where you headed?" Jonah's mouth is stuffed with cake. He can't go with me, not just yet, I tell him, admiring his new Satchel Paige baseball card.

In the doorway, I wave at Bessie across the street, holding her new baby brother. Passing grown-ups on the porch, I look at them smile at me. The whole town is talking about the banker passing for white and killing to keep his secrets. Negroes do not know what to make of it all. "A soldier trying to kill our babies," Mrs. Ruby says. "Disgraceful. After what so many of them did to lift us up and bring credit to us all."

Mrs. Loewenthal says, "Oh, what they must be saying in the synagogues."

The mayor wants to give me a medal. I cannot accept it, I told him. It's all wrapped in too much sadness for me. Both the Negroes and the whites are saying it this time. I do not know my place, turning down the mayor for an honor like this. Auntie simply winks at me and says she doesn't know what will ever become of me.

When I am almost at the graveyard, I stop. Making a fan out of orange and red leaves, I carry them inside. "You, gal. Octobia May. How's the day treating you, girlie?"

Standing at the gate, I stop and talk to Officer O'Malley. He is back on duty. Sometimes he even stops by the house just to see me. "You saved my life," he told me right before they rescued us on the river. "I'm indebted to you, you know."

A white man admitting to owing a Negro girl; Mr. Buster said he never figured to live long enough to hear a thing like that.

"The hearing will be coming up soon for those two, lassie. They'll want you and the boy to testify. Me, as well." He takes his hat off and sticks it underneath his arm. "Will you be brave enough to do that? Tell what a colored man did?"

I was born brave, I tell him. Then I ask about the day on the boat. "When you were upset. I heard you almost say. You said . . ." The word begins with an *n* and ends with an *r*, I tell him. I do not say the word because I do not like the word. "Why did you use it?" I ask. "My parents. Auntie. They say you disgrace yourself if you do."

"I . . . I . . . I . . ." He says he doesn't remember saying it. "But when people act . . ." He scratches his head. "Those fellas are less than . . ." He asks me why I am staring at him so. "Girlie. I tell you. My life is a wreck since you've walked into it." He paces like Mr. Harrison on the boat. "Men with guns. Negro girls biting white officers. Grown men at the station taunting me. They think I let the likes of you get the better of me. How can I live that down?"

I quiet the dry leaves in my hands and look into his face awhile. "I hear my friends calling me. I have to go," I say, stepping away from the fence. I think he wants to talk some more, but this is Auntie's special day. I'll have to be getting back soon.

"Well, listen up, child. Be on the lookout for . . . vampires and such in there. Now hear me?"

"Yes, sir."

"I do not want to have to come and rescue you."

Officer O'Malley walks up the street, twirling his nightstick while he whistles.

I am whistling, too. And thinking about the money that I rescued from Mr. Davenport. Bessie and I think Mr. Thurgood Marshall and the NAACP will make good use of that.

Feeling Auntie's dress pull leaves up the path behind me, I make my way uphill. I am not far along, though, when a girl screams, "Help! Somebody. Please."

I am running as fast as I can. Dropping leaves. Stopping, I apologize to Juppie and the girls. "I can't visit," I say, "someone is in big trouble. I have to save them. Hold on. I'm — I'm coming," I say, freeing myself from the dress. Glad I kept on my shirt and pants, I climb a tall hill. Stopping at the top, my hand above my eyes like a visor, I can see clear back to Auntie's place. With a long stick in my hand, I yell with all my might. "Charge!"

SELECTED BIBLIOGRAPHY

BOOKS:

Blaustein, Albert P., and Clarence Clyde Ferguson, Jr. *Desegregation and the Law: The Meaning and Effect of the School Desegregation Cases.* New Brunswick, NJ: Rutgers University Press, 1957.

Buchanan, A. Russell. *Black Americans in World War II.* Santa Barbara, CA: Clio Books, 1977.

Carter, Allene G., and Robert L. Allen. *Honoring Sergeant Carter: A Family's Journey to Uncover the Truth About an American Hero.* New York: Amistad, 2003.

Edgcomb, Gabrielle Simon. *From Swastika to Jim Crow: Refugee Scholars at Black Colleges.* Malabar, FL: Krieger Publishing Company, 1993.

Motley, Mary Penick, editor. *The Invisible Soldier: The Experience of the Black Soldier, World War II.* Detroit: Wayne State University Press, 1987.

ADDITIONAL SOURCES:

" 'EE' Fund Over $11,000 Mark," *The Courier,* November 28, 1953.

"Emerging from History: Massacre of 11 Black Soldiers," *USA Today,* November 8, 2013.

"October 12 Is EE Day: Will We Face the Challenge?" *The Courier*, June 20, 1953, national edition, page 1.

"Nation Set for Big Day," *The Courier*, November 28, 1953, Carolina Edition, page 1.

"Negro Jobs in White Banks," *Ebony*, December 1, 1951.

"Segregated Schools Doomed, South Told!" *The Courier*, June 20, 1953, national edition, page 1.

SPECIAL THANKS TO:

My father, Henry Flake, and my sister, Veronica Flake

Rachel Kranson, Professor of Jewish History, University of Pittsburgh

Carnegie Library of Pittsburgh

National Museum of American Jewish History

ACKNOWLEDGMENTS

Thank you to the Carnegie Library of Pittsburgh, where I spent countless hours going through newspapers, magazines, and photographs in an effort to learn about events and times none of us should ever forget. Thanks to my father, Henry Flake, my mother, Roberta Flake, and my sister, Veronica Flake, whose recall of the 1950s was remarkable and helpful in grounding the novel in the past.

Gratitude goes to Mr. Buster, whose name I use here (but not his persona or likeness) as a symbol of the love and pride I always felt growing up in North Philadelphia and of our friendship during my adult years; to Rachel Kranson, Professor of Jewish History at the University of Pittsburgh, for taking the time to read the manuscript. Your keen eye and expertise were much appreciated. Thank you to the African American World War II soldiers and veterans who fought for freedom in the military and at home.

Thanks also to *The Courier*, which played a significant role in the fight for social justice in America, especially during World World II and later when African Americans were striking a blow for freedom and equality everywhere. Special thanks to the Philadelphia Holocaust Awareness Museum and Education Center, where the exhibition on refugee scholars at historically black colleges led to the re-creation of my character Mrs. Lowenthal; to the NAACP and Mr. Thurgood Marshall, who fearlessly fought for the rights of millions of African Americans, thereby helping to uproot Jim Crow's stranglehold on America and usher our nation forward.

To Linda Pratt, my agent and friend. Part of the fun of walking this journey has been traveling it along with you. Through laughter and tears you have always believed and given the best wisdom and advice. So glad to have you by my side.

To Andrea Davis Pinkney, my editor and the woman who first discovered me. Words have not been written that could express how much you've meant to me and my career. From *The Skin I'm In* to *Pinned* and now *Unstoppable Octobia May*, it has been one wild and wondrous ride. You are most remarkable. Thanks so much for all you've done for me and the entire field of children's literature. Neither one of us would be the same without you.

To my Scholastic family, who makes me feel so at home. Thanks a million for everything.

Thanks to author Tonya Bolden for the title of this book and those so cool talks we have from time to time.

Blessings and love.

Sharon G. Flake is the author of many acclaimed books for young readers, including *The Skin I'm In* and *Pinned*, which was an NAACP Image Award nominee. Ms. Flake's writing has been hailed in multiple starred reviews as "brilliantly realized," "authentic," and "complex."

Ms. Flake has received three Coretta Scott King Author Honor Award citations and has been named the voice of middle-grade youth and an author to watch by *Publishers Weekly* magazine. Ms. Flake lives in Pittsburgh, Pennsylvania.

Please visit Sharon G. Flake on her website, www .sharongflake.com, and on Facebook and Twitter.